The Billionaire's Voice

THE SINCLAIRS

ALSO BY J.S. SCOTT

The Sinclairs

The Billionaire's Christmas (A Sinclair Novella)
No Ordinary Billionaire
The Forbidden Billionaire
The Billionaire's Touch

The Billionaire's Obsession

Mine for Tonight
Mine for Now
Mine Forever
Mine Completely
Heart of the Billionaire – Sam
Billionaire Undone – Travis
The Billionaire's Salvation – Max
The Billionaire's Game – Kade
Billionaire Unmasked – Jason
Billionaire Untamed – Tate
Billionaire Undaunted – Zane

The Walker Brothers

Release!

The Sentinel Demons

A Dangerous Bargain
A Dangerous Hunger
A Dangerous Fury

Big Girls and Bad Boys

The Curve Ball
The Beast Loves Curves
Curves by Design
The Pleasure of His Punishment: Stories

The Changeling Encounters

Mate of the Werewolf
The Dangers of Adopting a Werewolf
All I Want for Christmas is a Werewolf

The Vampire Coalition

Ethan's Mate
Rory's Mate
Nathan's Mate
Liam's Mate
Daric's Mate

The Billionaire's Voice

THE SINCLAIRS

J.S. Scott

Published by Montlake Romance, Seattle

www.apub.com

Amazon, the Amazon logo, and Montlake Romance are trademarks of Amazon.com, Inc., or its affiliates.

ISBN-13: 9781503936652
ISBN-10: 1503936651

Cover design by Laura Klynstra
Cover photography by Laura Klynstra

Printed in the United States of America

I think there has been a time in almost everyone's life where they've experienced too many tragedies or disappointments in too short of a length of time. Or maybe losses so grave that it knocks them so far down that they don't feel like they can ever get up again. Our lives are full of highs and lows, but sometimes there are those really seemingly hopeless periods of time that seem almost impossible to overcome, when it feels like one more blow will destroy you completely.
For anyone who has had to overcome one of those very dark, lonely, painful times, this book is for you.

- Jan

PROLOGUE

Tessa Sullivan rushed out of the fancy Boston restaurant, her vision blurred with unshed tears. She was so gutted that she stepped off the curb distractedly, startled when a strong, masculine hand grabbed her arm.

Her head jerked around and she tilted her chin to look up—way up—at a man she'd never seen before.

"The traffic is busy tonight, and I was afraid you were going to keep walking. You look like you're in another place. It's hard to believe you didn't hear the traffic. You must be really distracted. I hope I didn't scare you. I'm sorry."

Honestly, she *might* have kept walking if he hadn't detained her. Her brain was so muddled, her world so silent that she couldn't hear the cars. "Thank you," she said quietly. "I'm deaf."

He was tall, broad, and he definitely had the "bad boy" look going on. But when he grinned at her, Tessa had a difficult time not smiling back. For as tough as he looked on the exterior, his eyes were kind.

"You read lips?" He let go of her arm slowly. She nodded as she took in his black leather jacket and the baseball cap he was wearing. She guessed he was a few years older than she was, but it was hard to really tell. There was spiky, dark hair escaping his hat, and his eyes were the color of milk chocolate and seemed very kind, which for her made him highly likable, since those eyes held an empathy and warmth that was more than welcome at the moment.

"You need a ride? My car is right across the street." He waved his arm at a limo sitting directly across from them.

She shook her head vigorously. "My fiancé's car—" She caught herself, her voice shaky. "I mean my *ex*-fiancé's car is here somewhere."

"You just broke up," the stranger guessed, his smile fading.

"Yes." She thought better about confessing her problems to a stranger and corrected herself. "No."

Then she looked into the eyes of her rescuer and wondered why she cared about telling anybody the truth. She had nothing to lose anymore. "Yes," she murmured sadly. "I'm sorry. I guess since it just happened, I'm not quite used to admitting I got dumped."

The big man took her hand. "No reason to ride with an asshole. Come with me."

Tessa let herself be led across the street before she had a chance to tell him that Rick wasn't going with her. A driver hopped out and opened the limo door for her as her mystery man jumped in on the other side.

Looking around frantically, she couldn't see Rick's car and driver anywhere. She hesitated like any normal woman would do when a stranger offers her a ride, but she was beyond being cautious. The guy had a driver as a chaperone, and she was fairly certain serial killers didn't ride in limos, at least not when they were going to commit a crime.

Tessa was still deciding what to do when a group of women across the street started to wave frantically at the car. It was obvious that they were screaming, trying to get the passenger's attention, but Tessa had no idea why.

Mr. Bad Boy leveraged his body across the backseat and stuck his head out the door so she could read his lips. "Get in or we're going to get mobbed. I'm recognizable, and I really don't want anybody to get hurt. Please."

His look was so persuasive and urgent that she jumped into the car without another thought, the driver hurrying to close her door and get the car in motion before the women could cross the busy street and descend on them.

The man turned on the light in the back of the limo. "We made it." The cap came off his head quickly and he raked his hands through his short, dark, spiky hair. After he discarded the jacket, too, he reclined back on the seat, still angled toward her.

Tessa couldn't help but be slightly amused by the relieved look on his face. "Your fan club?" she questioned teasingly.

"Actually, yeah. A few of them, anyway." He looked at her curiously. "You still don't recognize me?"

He was wearing a T-shirt, and she could see now that he had some very ornate tattoos on his biceps. She generally didn't care for tats on a guy, but somehow they suited him, and they weren't done up to the point of overkill. "No. I really don't. Should I?"

"My name is Xander. I'm a musician. We're performing here in Boston tomorrow night to a sold-out crowd. Our first album sold millions. I'm working on our next one."

Tessa pointed at her ear. "Deaf. Remember? I don't keep up with the music trends much. Besides, I'm a classical-music kind of woman."

"How do you know I'm not a classical artist?" he retorted.

She looked him up and down a few times. "Okay. Maybe I'm stereotyping, but you look like a rocker. I'm sorry. Do you perform classical? If you do, I'm not familiar with your work." As an afterthought, she told him, "My name is Tessa, by the way." She was a little surprised that he didn't recognize her, either, but the two of them were obviously worlds apart.

He grinned mischievously. "Hell, no. I like all types of music, but I like to rock the house."

He asked where she wanted to go, and Xander made arrangements with the driver before closing the window between them again.

"So some idiot dumped you tonight, Tessa?" he asked once he had leaned back in his seat again. "Why?"

Before she knew it, Tessa was blurting out the entire story of her and Rick's breakup, and some of the events leading to the split.

"What an asshole," Xander commented as she turned into a blubbering idiot. He moved closer and put a comforting hand on her shoulder.

She continued to sob. "He's right. Things have changed. He signed up for the *old me*, not the *deaf me*."

He moved back a little and looked down so she could see his face. "Don't you fucking dare make excuses for him. When you love somebody, you love the whole person. Losing your hearing shouldn't have made a damn bit of difference. Yeah. I'd be sad if somebody I loved had something happen to make their life more difficult, but you don't just fall out of love. I think real love grabs a guy by the balls and never lets him go. Superficial shit shouldn't matter."

Tessa wouldn't exactly call losing one of her important senses superficial, but Xander was validating what she thought love should be. "I think so, too," she answered softly.

Xander squeezed her shoulder. "He wasn't the right one. Someday, you'll grab a man's nuts and he'll do anything to keep you."

Tessa snorted. Xander said whatever he thought in a pretty blunt way, but she was starting to like that about him. Obviously, there were tons of other women in the world who liked him that way, too.

By the time they pulled up in front of Rick's house, Tessa was feeling more together. Somehow, Xander had made her feel slightly better—in his own unique way.

"Where will you go?" he asked as the car pulled to a stop.

"Home," she said adamantly. "I think it's time I find out who I really am." She needed to find herself again after losing who she really was to be the woman Rick wanted. She was beginning to understand that, somewhere along the way, she'd lost herself.

"Where is home?"

"Amesport, Maine. It's a small coastal town. My parents still live there."

Xander shrugged his wide shoulders. "Sounds like as good a place as any to find a good guy."

She smiled at him. "I need to find myself first." Impulsively, she leaned over and hugged him.

The friendly embrace wasn't awkward. In fact, Xander squeezed her tightly before he finally let her go, and Tessa savored the moment of human connection.

"Thank you," she murmured as the door of the limo opened, the driver standing outside waiting for her to get out.

Xander put a detaining hand on her forearm. "Don't take any shit from anybody, Tessa. Not ever. You're a beautiful woman. Any guy would be lucky to have you. Remember that. Find out who you are before you choose your next guy. Let him love the real you."

She nodded, getting teary-eyed as she got her last glimpse of his earnest face, touched that a complete stranger, a rock star, had listened to her woes and helped her, even though he didn't even know her.

It was enough to almost restore her faith in the goodness of people.

"Good luck with the concert. Keep rocking the houses," she told him with a sniffle.

"You know it," he answered with a cocky smirk. "We always do."

Her heart was just a little bit lighter as she watched the limo leave. It had been a strange encounter, but he'd made an impact on her life when she'd really needed a friendly acquaintance. It had been a positive experience, one of the first she'd had in quite some time, and she knew she'd never forget it.

Her packing didn't take long. The messaging to her parents wasn't easy, but when she left the next morning, Tessa found herself looking forward to going home.

She left the key to the mansion and her enormous diamond on Rick's bedside table.

He had never come home, so she hadn't needed to see him again.

The cabbie helped her stow her bags, and Tessa never looked back as they headed down the driveway.

She cried all the way to the airport, her fear of an unknown future and her disappointed hopes still tearing her apart. By the time she got to her terminal, she couldn't weep anymore. Rick had broken her, but after a sleepless night, she realized that she'd get over being thrown aside because she was damaged.

He isn't worth crying about anymore.

Tessa left Boston behind her and buried her pain, determined to find contentment in the small, quirky coastal town she'd always loved.

CHAPTER 1

The Present . . .

One thing she really hated about being deaf was that the only sounds she could ever hear when she was alone were her own thoughts.

Tessa Sullivan let out a contented sigh as the hot water from the shower pulsated over her naked body. Having just finished her morning run, there was no better sensation than feeling her taut muscles relaxing as the single jet above her head released a steady spray of warmth. Even though she'd gotten overheated during her jog, the cleansing heat still felt glorious.

"I'm out of shape," she mumbled to herself, remembering how badly she had been panting after her three-mile jaunt. Skipping some of her exercise routine over the busy summer had really cost her. Tessa sighed as she realized it was going to take her a while to get back to her pre-summer distance running.

Strangely, she *still* talked to herself, even though she couldn't hear. Old habits died hard, and she'd always chattered away, even as a child, whether anyone was listening or not.

Maybe she spoke out loud because it made her feel less isolated. Being deaf was lonely sometimes, and even if she couldn't hear herself speak, her ramblings kept her company.

She soaped her body in silence, letting herself absorb a sense of peace that flowed over her soul, an experience that was occurring more and more often lately. For years, she'd lamented the loss of her hearing. Now, she was finally beginning to accept the fact that voices and noise weren't part of her life. Tessa knew she'd always miss the sense of sound, but she'd finally realized that being deaf hadn't changed who she was.

I'm still . . . me. I've just learned how to interpret the world around me differently.

Every person had a voice, whether or not she could remember how that individual had sounded before, or even if she'd never met them before she'd lost her hearing. As she watched a person speak or sign, she could hear that unique voice, a sound in her head and a feeling she identified with a certain individual.

She rinsed her hair leisurely, glad that summer was finally over. The restaurant that she owned with her brother, Liam, would be slower, but she looked forward to the less frantic pace of the fall in Amesport. Labor Day had just passed, and the atmosphere of the Maine coastal town would change from one of tourist madness back to the small, friendly town she adored. Summer was fun, crazy, and frantic from all the visitors; fall was a season that most of the locals loved because many of the tourists had gone home.

The house still hasn't sold.

Selfishly, she was glad that Randi's old home hadn't sold over the summer, though she felt guilty for having those thoughts. Her friend needed to eventually sell her house, even though she'd married a billionaire. In the meantime, Tessa was enjoying the solitude of playing caretaker for the small, single-family ranch home on a few acres of property outside of town. It gave her some much-needed space from Liam, her protective sibling and business partner.

I'm going to need to talk to Liam . . . again.

She'd gone deaf over six years ago, but her brother still treated her like she was delicate, fragile. He blamed himself for her lack of hearing, even though it had been far from his fault. He seemed determined to keep her safe, but his machinations went way too far. Tessa felt suffocated. She was twenty-seven, far too old to need a babysitter. She knew Liam meant well, but he was going to have to let her go eventually. He'd given up enough to take care of her, stay supportively by her side for so many years. It was time for him to live his own life again, and way past time for her to take control of her own.

The water turned off soundlessly as she pushed the handle and stood in the enclosure for a moment to wring out her hair. As she stepped out, Tessa reached for the clean towel she'd tossed on the hamper next to the shower, only to find that it wasn't there.

A shriek of startled fear left her mouth as she turned and saw a very large, very male hand holding out the missing sky-blue towel. Her eyes flew to his face as she screamed, recognizing the intruder.

"Oh, my God. What in the hell are you doing here?" she asked Micah Sinclair as he slowly released his grip on the towel when she reached for it shakily, not bothering to hide the heat in his dark-brown eyes as he stared shamelessly at her nude body. Finally, she jerked on the material hard, freeing the towel from his reluctantly loose grip.

A fiery blush flooded her face and body as she quickly wrapped it around her, wishing she'd grabbed one of the larger, fluffier ones in the closet for her shower, but she didn't want to use Randi's nicer stuff. As it was, the threadbare cotton piece of linen she'd chosen barely covered her ass and other private areas she didn't want exposed. She had no choice but to look at Micah—even though she was mortified—if she wanted to know his response.

His eyes were both hungry and mischievous, a combination that was nearly irresistible.

"I could ask you the same." He answered slowly, signing with American Sign Language—ASL for short—as he spoke. "Not that I mind. Now we've both seen the other one naked."

Deep, silky smooth, and sinful. That was how she *heard* Micah's *voice.* She had since the minute she'd met him.

Tessa was good at reading lips, but she found it much easier with people she knew well. Although Micah wasn't exactly a stranger, she'd *always* been able to understand him, for some reason. She'd been able to pick up the majority of his words from their very first encounter, which had been in a very similarly embarrassing way—except *he* had been the one standing in a bathroom naked, a tantalizing sight that Tessa had never been able to erase from her brain—no matter how much she tried. "I'm caretaking the house," she told him hastily, trying to pull the towel more snugly around her body. "I moved in several months ago. After Evan and Randi's wedding. What are you doing here?"

She shivered, but she wasn't really cold. The warmth in Micah's eyes was enough to heat the small home for an entire Maine winter. But there was something about him that looked . . . different.

Micah Sinclair was usually cocky, a trait that the Sinclair men shared. Not rude, exactly, but Tessa was starting to think it was a behavior that every Sinclair male had acquired at birth. Every one of them exuded almost an obnoxious confidence that could also be perceived as arrogant.

Silently, her eyes moved over him, taking in every detail. He was dressed casually in a pair of jeans that had softened and faded with age, and hugged his body lovingly. The T-shirt he was wearing probably dated back to his college days, the blue fabric sporting the logo of an Ivy League school. It wasn't his clothing that seemed . . . off; it was something else that seemed different. It wasn't strange to see him in comfortable clothing. Other than his formal dress for Evan's wedding and Hope's winter party, Tessa had noticed that he wasn't a fancy dresser, even though he was no less wealthy than his brothers or cousins.

Usually, he appeared to be a rugged, outdoorsy kind of guy. Probably because that was exactly what he was: an extreme-sports mogul. But today he wasn't exuding the same barely containable energy he usually did.

He looks . . . exhausted.

She studied his face again, noticing the weary look and the dark circles beneath his eyes.

"I bought the house," he announced suddenly.

Tessa was glad Micah had signed along with his statement, because she'd been so preoccupied with his eyes that she hadn't looked at his lips. "This house?" she squeaked.

He nodded.

"How is that possible? Randi didn't tell me, and she and Evan are away in the Orient for a belated honeymoon." Her friend would be gone for several more weeks, and she hadn't texted Tessa for several days. Surely Randi would have let her know the house had sold so she could get out before the new owner arrived.

Micah grinned at her, making him suddenly seem much more approachable. "It was a quick deal. Evan and Randi are under the impression that I'm not taking possession for a while. They wouldn't have wanted you to leave."

"Then why are you here?" she asked, feeling uncomfortable standing in the bathroom with only a towel wrapped around her body while she conversed with the hottest guy she'd ever met.

Honestly, it was pretty humiliating.

He shrugged. "Spontaneous trip. I decided to check out the property once the deal closed."

Tessa knew instinctively that his decision to come here wasn't completely on a whim. She might not be able to hear, but her other senses and her instincts were sharp, and she could feel that something wasn't quite right. "And did you check out the property?" she asked, feeling awkward.

"Not all of it. I didn't just buy this place. I purchased several other parcels that are connected to this property. That's a lot of acreage to see." He paused before adding, "I'm actually rather glad I decided to check out the house first. My timing was excellent."

He was teasing her, but she still blushed all over again. "I'm not glad you're here. I'm naked," she replied bluntly.

"Unfortunately for me, you aren't anymore." His grin grew broader, and his eyes caressed her devilishly.

He's flirting.

The thought made her feel dumbfounded, even though she was sure that Micah probably flirted with every woman he met. Men didn't look at her as a sexual creature. She was deaf, disabled as far as most males were concerned. Guys might like her as a friend, but they did not look at her like she was the hottest female on the East Coast. Except . . . for some reason . . . this man did.

"I need to get dressed," Tessa mumbled, trying to make her way around Micah Sinclair's muscular body blocking the entrance to the small bathroom. The air in the room was getting electric with sexual tension and it made her uncomfortable, especially since the real attraction was probably all coming from her.

He caught her bare upper arm and tilted her face up to look at him. "Tessa?"

She felt her heart skitter as she inhaled his intoxicatingly masculine scent. He was too close, so close that she could feel the heat of his body, pressed up against his hip.

"Yes?" she choked out, wanting to escape the small room that suddenly felt much too warm and much too small.

"I didn't mean to scare you. I'm sorry." He didn't sign this time, but she caught his words.

"If what you're saying is true, *I'm* the one invading *your* privacy," she reminded him, her gaze staying on his lips because he wasn't signing. "I wish I had known the property had sold. I would have left right away."

"You're not intruding. In fact, seeing you here is the best thing that's happened to me in a while."

Damn. He must be desperate for entertainment if seeing me here in his new property is actually a good thing.

Not knowing what to say, she scrambled around him and pulled her arm from his grasp. "I'll go as soon as I can," she told him hastily as she darted out of the bathroom.

"I hope not." Micah smiled at her departing figure, his soft, low comment going unheard and unnoticed by the fleeing woman.

In some ways, it had been instinct that had brought Micah here to Amesport. Granted, rest and relaxation had been the doctor's orders, but when his physician had told him that he needed a total hiatus, the first place he'd thought about was all of his new property in Maine.

When he said he'd acquired a lot of acreage . . . he meant it. Much of the wooded property on this side of town, outside the city limits, now belonged to him. The empty lots along the coastline had been the most difficult and expensive to purchase. They had been owned by an out-of-town contractor who had wanted to build on the coastline when the economy improved. All it had taken to change the man's mind was more money and some bargaining discussions. After watching the guy, Micah knew just how much to offer to make him cave in and give up the property. Buying Randi's old house away from the coast had been an afterthought, a way to help Randi and to give Micah a home that could one day house a caretaker for the massive amount of acreage he now owned.

Seating himself on the living-room couch while he waited for Tessa, Micah rubbed his forehead as he remembered how he'd been determined to ignore his doctor's advice. The last thing he needed was time away from his company. Then, he'd had another debilitating incident even worse than the last. That had been enough to make him consider taking a short trip away from the city.

I've gone without an episode for years. Why now?

According to his doctor in New York, the reasons were endless: his stress over his youngest brother, Xander; too much caffeine; too little sleep; too much travel; not eating right; etc., etc. Even though it had nearly killed him to hand over the daily running of his company to his executives, he'd done it. There was no denying that his temper was getting short, and that he wasn't concentrating well. When his long-ago-and-never-thought-about episodes had returned with a vengeance, he'd finally admitted that he needed . . . something.

Leaning back on the comfortable old sofa, Micah confessed silently that just flying himself here had been a release that he hadn't experienced for a long time. He'd recently acquired a Cessna, and piloting himself to Maine had reminded him how much he missed the exhilaration of being alone, just him and an endless expanse of sky.

Finding Tessa here had been another plus, but he was cursing his unruly cock as it pressed against the unyielding denim of his jeans.

She's just as beautiful as I remember!

As if he'd ever forget her staring at him like he was some kind of apparition when he'd stepped out of the shower at Jared's guesthouse, the first time they'd met? Her expression had turned from one of terror to mortification, then finally curiosity as she'd surveyed his body. Shit, he still got wood just thinking about her fascinated gaze.

For some reason, Tessa had intrigued him from day one, and his preoccupation with her intensified after every encounter they had.

He'd gotten very little opportunity to talk to her during Evan's wedding. Micah had been the only Sinclair cousin who had made it to

Amesport for the official union between Evan and Miranda "Randi" Tyler. Julian had been in the middle of shooting a film out of country, and Xander was in no shape to travel. Regrettably, Micah had needed to leave right after the reception, and had only exchanged a few words with Tessa that day.

But that doesn't mean I haven't thought about her.

He thought about her too damn much for his liking.

Being back in Amesport felt good, real. He'd tried lying to himself when he'd bought Randi's old home and much of the surrounding area, adamantly putting the notion in his brain that it would be a good buy from a business perspective. *Okay, yeah,* it probably *would* be a good investment since the town was growing. Maybe if he wanted to commercially build up the area he'd bought, it might even be reasonable. His cousin Jared had married a woman who had a steadily growing business in Amesport, and Randi's special-learning-needs school would probably open next year. Eventually, the town would expand and grow. The speculation would make sense. But that *wasn't* the reason he'd bought up the land. He was bullshitting himself, trying to rationalize the unreasonable. In reality, his reasons were far more personal.

His cock went stiff again as Tessa came out of the bedroom looking breathless and rumpled.

On her, the just-rolled-out-of-bed look was incredibly sensual. He wondered if that's how she'd look after she came for him, and the desire to find out was nearly overwhelming.

Micah groaned inwardly as he noticed the perfectly modest shorts and the red T-shirt she was wearing. Her hair was probably still drying, but the plump curls were already visible, making him want to bury his fingers into the blonde, disorderly, spiraled locks to see if they were as soft and silky as they looked. On closer scrutiny, he didn't see any makeup on her face, but her skin was glowing. The light-green eyes looking at him expectantly nearly did him in. The feeling that he'd seen her face before he'd ever met her hammered at him once again. She'd always looked familiar, but maybe he just fucking *wanted* to know her.

He wanted Tessa Sullivan—had from the first time he'd seen her, and the desire to bury himself inside her was getting impossible to ignore. Hell, he thought about her all the time, and she haunted his very dirty dreams even though he barely knew her. Honestly, he knew that *she* was one of the reasons he was here. He needed to get over his crazy obsession with the petite blonde, spend enough time with her to realize that his fantasies were nothing like reality. Micah was convinced that once he got to know Tessa, his fascination with her would stop tormenting him all the way to New York.

The way she was staring at his lips was oddly erotic, even though he knew exactly why her gaze was fixed on his mouth. He cursed himself for getting turned on by an action that was strictly necessity for her.

"I'm ready. I don't really have much. I stored my stuff in Liam's garage and just brought what I needed. I knew I wouldn't be here forever," she told him softly.

Micah signed as he spoke. "You gave up your apartment?"

He was secretly glad he'd brushed up on his ASL. There was no question as to *why* he'd done it. Micah wasn't going to lie to himself anymore, or deny that his dick got hard over seeing Tessa. Truth was . . . he wanted to be able to communicate with her without looking awkward, and he just wanted to get over whatever madness Tessa Sullivan had driven him into. He was sick of his cock popping up like a jack-in-the-box every damn time he thought about her.

Now, he knew seeing her in person wasn't helping. It was making his embarrassing condition even worse.

She nodded. "I wanted to save money over the summer, and rentals are outrageous. The price triples during tourist months."

Micah knew she cleaned for his Sinclair cousins—who lived out on the exclusive Amesport Peninsula—during the winter months when the restaurant she owned with Liam was slower. Obviously, she was also willing to watch homes while the owners were absent. "Don't you have to drive to the restaurant every day?"

"Not every day after the summer months," she answered. "Our open hours are shorter, and we're closed more days. We have staff that we want to keep even though they'll work less hours. Liam handles most of the management at the restaurant during the winter, and he's anal about the way things are run there. I just work the busy days, and cover for other staff when they need me."

"So where will you go if you leave here? Are your parents still alive?"

"No," Tessa answered sadly. "They're both gone, but Liam lives in my parents' old home. I'll move back in with him. I have to try and earn more money this winter. We need to have the restaurant renovated."

Micah had already run into Tessa's obsessively protective brother. He could understand why she didn't look happy about being house-mates with her only sibling. He'd been to Sullivan's Steak and Seafood for dinner, and the food was spectacular. However, the shack near the end of the pier was badly in need of repair, so he could also understand why Tessa was saving.

"You were hoping to stay here for the winter, weren't you?" He automatically signed as he spoke.

"Hoping," she confided. "But I knew the house could sell at any time."

"Do you have more jobs lined up?" he asked curiously.

"Just the cleaning services on the Peninsula, but I think I can find more jobs. I just started looking." She fidgeted, and her eyes looked troubled.

Micah stood. "Then don't leave, Tessa. Stay here. It's not like I'll be here long, and I'll need somebody to watch the property." The words left his lips impulsively, but Micah knew he'd never wanted anything more. Tessa wanted work, and he wanted to give it to her . . . in more ways than one.

What faster way was there to get to know a person than if they were living in a house that he owned, that he could visit whenever he wanted? It was a perfect situation, and Micah wasn't the kind of guy to miss out on an opportunity.

Life was too damn short, and he wanted to shake off his desperation to fuck Tessa Sullivan once and for all.

CHAPTER 2

"What? Stay here? Why?" Micah had signed it. He'd spoken the words. Still, Tessa couldn't quite believe that she completely understood what he was asking her to do.

"I want you to stay. I'll be here in Amesport for a few weeks, but I'll put myself up in Jared's guesthouse. You can still function as a caretaker. I could use some help finding my way around. I don't know the area or the property. And I'll need someone to watch my property when I leave."

Oh, God. I can't stay here now that the house belongs to him.

Not only was it ridiculous to think he needed help, but she knew Liam would go ballistic. Her brother had mentioned that he thought Micah found her attractive, and he'd made it totally clear to her that she needed to stay away from this particular Sinclair. She'd rolled her eyes at her brother and walked away. *Like some billionaire Sinclair was going to be sexually into me?* She had been a little concerned that Liam was delusional. Micah might flirt, but Tessa had no doubt that he flattered every woman he came in contact with, even the deaf ones.

"I'm willing to pay you very well," he remarked casually. "Now that the property belongs to me, it's my responsibility to pay a caretaker. It's a lot of land. I'll need somebody who will stay on after I go."

He named a monthly figure that made Tessa go weak in the knees. Even if he only kept her through the winter, it would help her do a lot to improve the restaurant. It had been in their family since her grandparents had started the eatery decades ago. The restaurant meant everything to her.

"My brother hates you," she admitted.

Micah grinned. "I know. But I'm not asking your brother. I'm asking you."

Liam wasn't her keeper, but he thought he was. She wasn't afraid of rebelling and doing as she liked. She was more concerned about not hurting her only sibling in some way. Her brother had been by her side when she'd gone deaf, and then again after their parents died. He hadn't been thrilled when she moved out of town to take care of Randi's house, but she knew he was ecstatic about one thing—her giving up her own apartment. It meant she'd eventually have to move back home with him after the house sold.

It's time for Liam to stop. I've been able to handle my situation for a while now. He has to realize that I don't need him to keep sacrificing his life for me.

"Okay. I'll stay." She said the words before she could stop them. Really, she *did* want to stay, and not just for the job.

Tessa desperately wanted to know what had really brought Micah here to Maine, and why he was looking so weary. Something was wrong. She could sense it. Unfortunately, her curiosity almost always got her into trouble.

"Good." He smiled, looking relieved.

"I could cook for you free of charge," she answered mischievously.

"I don't expect you to cook."

She winked at him. "I like to eat and you're paying me well, so I'll cook when you're around. Are you hungry?"

He nodded slowly. "Honestly . . . yeah. I didn't have anything except coffee this morning. I was eager to get up in the air. We're supposed to have thunderstorms later and I flew myself in a Cessna."

Why am I not surprised that he's a pilot?

Really, flying was probably one of his tamer activities.

She busied herself by moving into the kitchen. Micah followed her. He took a seat at the small table after he asked if he could do anything and she refused his help. Working in a kitchen was something that came as naturally to her as breathing. Turning her back on him to make coffee, she wondered what he was thinking. If there was one thing that was still disconcerting about being deaf, it was the isolation she felt when someone was in the same room unless she was looking at that person directly. As she worked, Tessa realized that the silence wasn't uncomfortable. In a way, she could *sense* Micah's presence, and she didn't feel alone even though she couldn't see him. It was an unusual sensation, and one she really hadn't experienced since she'd lost her hearing.

Focusing on the task at hand, she had breakfast ready quickly. She didn't notice what Micah was occupying his time with until she had put their coffee and plates on the table.

"That's private," she growled, snatching a piece of paper from his fingers. "Do you always read other people's mail?"

He looked up at her. "Only when it has the logo of my charity on the correspondence. Technically, it's my mail, too."

It didn't take her long to bury the letter in a kitchen drawer and slam it closed. She should have tossed the silly offer a week ago. The missive *did* have the Sinclair Fund's name on the letterhead, but she was still ticked that he had picked it up and was in the process of reading it when she'd taken it away from him.

"It's addressed to me," she told him defensively, folding her arms across her chest.

"I should have recognized you," he said, eyeing Tessa curiously now. "You're Theresa Sullivan. I could never place your face, but I knew I'd seen you before. I've seen you skate."

It was no surprise that he hadn't known where he'd seen her previously. Almost nobody connected her previous life with the one she lived now. The Olympic gold medalist in figure skating from almost a decade ago was long gone. Who would know her now? The disabled deaf woman who helped run a broken-down restaurant in a small coastal town was very different from the eighteen-year-old young woman who'd once shined as a rising star. There was no fancy costume, no heavy makeup, and her hair was a tangled mess that she rarely bothered to try to contain in any sense of style anymore. She looked nothing like she had when she was skating competitively.

Tessa turned her back to him again, nervously fiddling with cutlery and napkins before setting them on the table.

"I'm not that woman anymore," she finally replied, seating herself across from him.

"Of course you are. You're still Theresa Sullivan, right?"

"Tessa," she told him tersely. "Everyone I know has always called me Tessa." Legally, her name *was* Theresa, but she'd only used it in competition and on legal documents.

"Okay, Tessa," he answered, still staring at her with a calculating look that almost scared her. Micah was no fool, and she knew he could sense her anger and frustration. "Are you going to do it?" He locked eyes with her for a moment, his expression curious.

Was he joking? "I can't. I'm deaf. I haven't skated since I lost my hearing."

The letter requesting her to perform in a reunion of past Olympic medalists had saddened her. She'd never be able to be the same woman she'd been ten years ago. Honestly, she wasn't certain how the Fund's committee had even learned of her whereabouts. Liam had shielded her, made sure to keep her out of the media. Outside of her circle of friends and some of the townspeople, nobody knew she'd once been one of the most accomplished figure skaters in the world. The small town of Amesport had kept her secret. It had grown over the last ten years, but the original residents had stayed silent, respected the fact that she was healing. Once she'd recovered, Rick had dumped her, and she'd come back home for good, her accident had been old news, and it really hadn't mattered anymore.

Micah shrugged as he took a slug of coffee and then dug into his eggs, bacon, and toast. "You could still do it."

She picked up her mug, but froze as she read his response. "I can't perform. I haven't skated in years, and I can't even hear the music. The Sinclair Fund obviously doesn't realize that I can't hear."

One other problem was that the event was taking place in New York City. Tessa was comfortable right here in Amesport. She didn't want to travel to New York.

Chewing on his toast, he stared at her for a long time before answering, "I didn't think you were the type of woman to give up easily."

He was calling her a quitter, and that pissed her off. "I'm retired from the sport. I had no choice. Deaf people don't do skating performances." She took a sip of her coffee, irritated that he was making it sound like she had any other option than to give up her skating career.

"The Fund is offering a very lucrative deal, and it's for a good cause."

Tessa felt tears of disappointment spring into her eyes, but she blinked them away as she sipped her coffee and then set the mug back on the table. It wasn't like she didn't *want* to do the appearance; it wasn't possible. They were offering good payment that she could desperately use, and all profits from the event were going to a children's charity that she really wanted to support.

A single tear escaped as she picked up her fork and attacked her eggs. Eating slowly, she avoided looking at his face.

She couldn't do it . . . period! Tessa didn't want to look at Micah and see his disappointed expression. It was clear to her that he really *did* think she could simply hit the ice and skate again. Maybe *he* had confidence in her, but she had none in herself when it came to doing the impossible. And she was almost angry at him for making it seem like performing again would be no big deal.

Maybe *he* could do anything, and thought nothing of risking his life by jumping from places that weren't made to be launch sites.

Maybe *he* was cocky enough to think that he was invincible.

She . . . wasn't.

The last thing she needed was to feel like a failure . . . again. Not when she was only now regaining control of her life.

Most of the time, she could forget who she'd been before she'd lost her hearing, but that stupid offer from the Sinclair Fund had temporarily brought it all rushing back with a vengeance. After her hearing loss, she'd put aside all thoughts of skating again. What was the point? It was a career path that she could never follow, and forgetting had been the sensible thing to do back then. She'd lost her fiancé over her handicap, and she'd taken a lot of emotional blows since she'd left Boston and the man she'd once worshipped.

After Tessa's father had passed away, her mother had needed help in the restaurant. When her mom had gotten sick, soon after her dad's death, and then died only a year later, Tessa had been thrust into the role of restaurant owner quickly. Liam had come home for good, giving up a well-loved, lucrative career to be here in Amesport with her. Back then, she'd needed her brother, had clung to him like a lifeline. Now, he was "helping her" until he drove her nearly insane.

It's time to move on. I'm finally content with my life now. I can't go back. I don't want to go back.

Finally, she answered, "You don't understand. You have no idea what it's like to suddenly lose everything you've ever known, everything you care about." She'd been incredibly isolated, suddenly handicapped, and unable to do the thing she'd loved most in the world.

She'd had so many losses over the course of five or six years that she hadn't been able to take another blow. She'd never had time to recover. Losing her hearing, her fiancé, her skating career, her father, and then finally her mom, all in a relatively short period of time, had nearly killed her.

Over time, she'd learned to function in a world with no sound. She was finally at peace with her condition. The last thing she needed was to reopen old wounds. She'd come too far to slide backward now.

There wasn't really a deaf community in her area, and she'd already had friends, so it had just been a matter of learning to connect with them again. The need to be able to communicate and not feel so isolated had been almost an obsession. She'd learned to read lips as quickly as possible when she was with Rick, and she'd become an expert at it from years of practice. ASL was easier, but other than Liam, her parents, and her best friend, Randi, nobody knew sign language. Becoming very, very good at lip reading had been her only option. And she *was* good at it, so good that some people didn't even notice she was deaf if she was having a face-to-face conversation with them.

Liam had told her that her speaking voice sounded almost identical to her pre-deafness voice. Her friends had claimed the same thing. But Tessa would never really know if they were pacifying her, or if what they said was the truth. It wasn't that she didn't trust them, but all of them had kind hearts, and what person who cared about her was going to tell a deaf woman that she talked strangely?

Slowly, she'd lost touch with most of her old friends in the area, feeling different from all of her former friends. It hurt to be different, but she'd learned to live with the distance between herself and old friends; most of them were still acquaintances, and they were kind to her.

Tessa startled as she felt the warmth of Micah's large, strong hand cradling hers. Her eyes flew to his face.

"I'll help you, Tessa." The look on his face was intense as he spoke. "You don't have to do it alone."

"I can't do it at all," she mumbled, unable to pull her hand from his. That simple contact warmed her, and the need for human connection was gnawing at her soul.

"Yes, you can. We danced, and you're still just as graceful as you ever were. You can feel the rhythm of music somehow. You must."

Actually, she really *didn't* hear whatever music was playing. She could sense vibrations. Once she understood the tempo, she matched a piece of music to that pace in her head. With Micah's confident lead, she'd been easily able to waltz with him. That night, the evening of Hope's ball last winter, had been a very memorable evening. She'd felt like Cinderella, and she'd never wanted to leave Micah's arms. Unfortunately, the dance had ended, but Tessa still hadn't forgotten the feel of his powerful body guiding her, immersing her in sensation.

Slowly, she shook her head. "I don't hear anything."

She explained how she was able to dance as Micah appeared to listen intently.

His grip on her fingers tightened. "I think you could manage to skate a routine the same way you danced," he told her, slipping his hand from hers to sign the words he was speaking.

The action had been unnecessary. Tessa had understood him, and her heart immediately started to ache from the lack of contact. "I can't," she insisted, unwilling to open a part of her life that needed to stay closed and in the past.

"Can't or won't?" he replied.

Micah was irritatingly persistent, and Tessa was starting to find the entire conversation uncomfortable. She didn't want to spill her guts to a guy she barely knew. Her lips started to curve into a smile as she considered the ironic fact that both of them knew what the other one looked like naked even though they'd exchanged very few words in the past. "Won't," she answered honestly.

"Why?" He looked genuinely perplexed now.

She could have answered his one-word question so many ways. The best answer was that she hadn't even tried to skate in almost a decade. She could claim that she was out of shape, which was true. Or she could try one more time to explain that she couldn't hear the music. Again, it wouldn't be a dishonest answer. She said none of those things.

"I'm scared," she blurted out impulsively, telling him the real reason she'd never touched a pair of skates again. Her life in the last several years had been depressing, full of painful emotional blows and losses. Getting on ice again and failing might very well finish her off, destroy her.

He shrugged. "I think that's natural. But you were the best in the world. Doing a simple routine would be a piece of cake. The Fund doesn't expect you to be perfect. All of the athletes invited to perform are *past* Olympians. They're all way past the age where they're in shape for competition."

Looking at him suspiciously, she asked, "I still haven't figured out how your charity found me. Did you tell them where to find me?"

"I didn't know who you were until I read that letter. I swear. I knew they were planning the event, but I didn't know you were involved."

"I'm not," she answered hurriedly.

"But you can be." He lifted an eyebrow in challenge.

Damn. Damn. Damn. There was nothing harder for her than to ignore a direct dare, and Micah *was* testing her. "It's not feasible. I have jobs to do."

He shook his head. "Not a good-enough reason. You wouldn't have to be in New York for more than a few days to perform, and you already admitted you aren't needed as much at the restaurant. Your responsibilities can be covered by somebody else."

"I'd only have six weeks to prepare. I can't get in shape in such a short amount of time, and I can't relearn skills I've probably long forgotten."

"You didn't forget; you've just buried the desire to get on skates again."

He was still spearing her with a knowing look, giving her the sense that he could almost look into her thoughts. Truth was, she *did* desperately want to skate again. It would be one less loss, one less gaping hole in her heart. When she'd given up the sport completely, it had left a very large void in her life.

The thought of trying and falling on her ass made her cringe. "You really *don't* understand," she muttered. "You're an athlete in prime condition. You have all of your senses. You're not operating with a disadvantage. It's easy to be courageous when you have nothing to fear."

"I understand that you're afraid of failure, but you won't fail. And you're wrong. My life isn't as perfect as you might think. I've had my ass in a desk chair for too long, and I'm not in great aerobic shape, but I'll work out with you. We'll do it together. I miss my runs."

Before she'd started up again a few weeks ago, Tessa had missed hers, too. She'd forgotten how much until she'd gotten outside every morning.

"*You* never fail at anything. You can't or you'd be dead." She didn't want to admit that some of the stunts he'd pulled off in the past fascinated and terrified her at the same time.

He frowned. "You're wrong again. I've failed at plenty of things. I've broken a lot of bones before I got it right sometimes, and now it seems I've lost my edge. My doctor ordered me out of my office."

"You're sick?" She looked again at his weary expression, concerned.

"No. According to my doctor I'm just . . . fatigued and burned out." He gave her a look that said he detested having *any* weaknesses. "Personally, I think he's full of shit, but I decided I could use a break. I can only be in an office for so long before I start going stir-crazy."

So *he* was hiding from the world, too. Tessa wanted to push him for more information, but his stony expression stopped her from asking any more questions. It was obvious that he didn't want to talk about it, so she went back to the original subject.

"There's a problem with your earlier suggestion," she told him confidently.

"What?"

"I can't practice. The rink my father helped build is closed. It went out of business several years ago, after he sold out his financial interest in the arena." Her dad had given up his share to his partners soon after she'd lost her hearing.

Micah smirked. "No problem." He dug into his pocket and pulled out his keys. "I'm not sure which one fits, but it seems I'm now the proud owner of one neglected skating rink."

Her heart starting pounding rapidly against the wall of her chest. The arena wasn't far from where Randi's house was located. Was it possible that he really *did* own the skating rink now, that he'd scooped up the closed building along with all of the property he'd recently acquired? It was highly probable, since the large acreage was for sale along with most of the other land outside the city limits in this direction.

Damn!

She looked at his attractive, grinning expression with alarm, and then stared at the keys he was now dangling between his large fingers.

If he was for real, she was screwed.

CHAPTER 3

Several days later, Micah finally took time out to consider if he was actually doing the right thing by nearly pushing Tessa back onto the ice. His instinct, his gut, told him that Tessa needed and wanted to skate again. But as she got ready to go practice for the first time, he was questioning his tactics. He'd dared her, cajoled her, and downright antagonized her for the last few days, not wanting her to give up the chance to discover that her skills hadn't gone away with her hearing.

He felt like a first-rate jerk, which he probably was, but he didn't want to actually admit it. He had basically continued to punch Tessa's buttons, challenged her until her pride probably demanded that she skate.

He collapsed on the couch with a protein drink in his hand, frowning as he thought about her confession that she hadn't skated in years. What if he was fucking wrong, what if his gut instinct was wrong? It could happen—although it generally didn't. He could have made all the wrong moves with her. Hell, he barely knew her.

She was afraid, and he'd come to realize in the last few days that there were very few things Tessa *couldn't* do. She was no shrinking violet, and, even though she was petite, she could nearly outrun him on the morning jogs they'd been doing since he'd arrived. They were pushing three miles at a rapid pace for aerobic exercise first, and his ass was dragging near the end of the run. Yeah, he'd kept up on his weight training, but he spent the majority of his time stressing over business and sitting in an office, and he'd made several unplanned trips to California thanks to Xander's erratic behavior. He'd been distracted, neglecting his cardio for the last several months. Now he was paying for it.

There was a time he could run marathon distances easily, but now a long-retired figure skater could nearly bust his balls. He wasn't happy about that.

Nevertheless, he had to admire Tessa's courage. Other than her reluctance to get back on the ice, she didn't let her lack of hearing keep her from doing anything a hearing person was able to do. She'd adapted, compensated by learning all of the skills necessary to be more than functional in a hearing world.

He admired her; he liked her.

Unfortunately, he *still* wanted to fuck her so badly that he could barely hold himself back. In fact, rather than curing his obsession, being close to her all the time was making his urgency worse. Every teasing smile she directed his way affected him and went directly to his cock. He didn't understand his reaction. Tessa was pretty, but he'd been with an uncounted number of gorgeous females since Anna had dumped him years ago. None of them had been able to turn him inside out with only a glance. Hell, he hadn't been this obsessed over Anna, and she'd been his girlfriend for several years, the woman he'd thought he'd end up with for the rest of his life.

What the fuck is wrong with me?

"I think I've . . . filled out." Tessa's unhappy voice sounded from the entrance to the living room.

Her words jerked Micah back into reality, and he looked up, nearly dropping the drink in his hand as he looked at her in a simple red skating skirt.

31

It was unadorned, a practice outfit, with long sleeves and a very high hem that left her slender legs bare. She had definitely grown in all the right places since she'd worn it years ago. The clingy material hugged a pair of full breasts that he was itching to touch, and curves that he wanted molded against his body. Except he'd prefer her naked and begging for him to make her come, those shapely legs wrapped around him as he pounded into her until they both came unglued.

"You look . . . fine," he answered gruffly.

You look like innocence and sin, sweet and sultry. You look like a goddamn elusive goddess that I need to capture and fuck before I lose my mind!

"You don't think it's too tight?" She spun around, yanking at the material clinging to her body.

He drained his glass, wishing it was something a hell of a lot stronger than gritty protein, watching her as she twirled around gracefully and tugged at the material that was lovingly hugging her curves. As he got a quick look at her shapely ass that was barely covered by the thin panties attached to the skirt, he nearly choked on the last swallow of liquid in his mouth.

Micah coughed, trying to cover up his rampant desire to take her by her perky ponytail and bend her over the nearest object so he could find relief from the constant hard-on he was sporting. In fact, he knew, after spending a few days in her company, that he wasn't going to get over his agitated insanity for her anytime soon.

Maybe the only cure was just to give in and try to seduce her. He should know by now that his erection wasn't going to go away until he was no longer enthralled by Tessa, and what he needed was to finally get bored and restless like he always did, before he could move on.

He coughed one last time before he spoke. "We can get you something new for the performance. It looks fine. Nobody will see you." *Thank God!* If any other guy started lusting after her like he was right now, which was what any guy with a pulse would do, Micah knew he'd want to choke the bastard on the spot.

"I'll get my skates," she said quietly, moving back toward the bedroom.

He released a breath he hadn't known he was holding as she disappeared into the other room. *Jesus!* How was he going to handle being close to her for much longer without fucking her senseless?

Was that a possessive thought he'd just had a few seconds ago? What the hell was that? He didn't do jealousy. He'd never realized it was even in his DNA.

Running a hand through his unruly hair, he contemplated leaving Maine, but that wasn't happening. The pull to be with Tessa was too strong, and there was much more involved in his attraction to her. Plus, he'd promised to be there for her so that she didn't have to face her fears alone. He wasn't letting his uncooperative dick and his desire to nail her interfere with a vow—a pledge he hadn't been able to keep himself from making, for some damn reason.

The problem was . . . he actually did *like* her. Tessa had a quirky sense of humor that made him laugh, and a sharp mind that made him think of things other than just business and his problems with his youngest brother. Tessa deserved better than a frantic fuck. He could tell the attraction went both ways, he could feel it, but he didn't want to hurt her. Sooner or later, he'd leave to go back to New York, and he'd already learned that he wasn't a "relationship" kind of guy. Tessa was the type of woman that a man didn't leave, and Micah was constantly on the go, always looking for his next adrenaline fix.

She needs a guy who cares about her, a man who will be by her side.

He stood, feeling antsy and irritated. Maybe Tessa needed a different sort of male in her life, but the thought of anyone except him touching her made him edgy as hell.

Dammit! Another possessive thought?

"I'm ready. Let's get this over with," Tessa said glumly as she entered the small living room again.

Her words made him smile as he turned in her direction, an automatic action that he didn't even think about anymore. "It won't be so bad." He signed as he spoke, even though he knew he didn't need to. It was rare that she didn't pick up enough of his words to understand him.

"I'm going to hate you for this," she warned.

Her words stopped Micah in his tracks. Maybe he *had* pushed too damn hard. Now he was beginning to second-guess his behavior, something he never did. He knew she was teasing, but was there some truth to what she'd said?

"Don't hate me," he said huskily, reaching out to tuck a stray spiral of her blonde hair behind her ear. "I think you want this, but you're too afraid to do it alone."

Her eyes locked with his, and Micah froze as he saw the vulnerability in her gaze. Feeling sucker punched as he stared into her unusual light-green eyes, he again began to question his motives and his actions. He sensed that Tessa needed to do this, but he felt like a bully for forcing her to do anything she didn't want to do. Honestly, all he wanted to do was wrap his arms protectively around her and keep her safe. Tessa had been through so much, suffered so many losses. Yet, she was more alive than any woman he'd ever known.

"I won't hate you. I promise," she answered softly, putting a hand on his forearm as he pulled his fingers away from her hair. "You're right. This is one last ghost from my past that I need to put to rest. Believe me, I wouldn't be trying this if part of me didn't really want to."

"Are you sure?" he asked, still feeling uncharacteristically uncertain.

She nodded slowly, and Micah felt himself relax. He captured her hand in his. "Then let's go." Suddenly, he wanted this first step to be over just as much as Tessa did.

"Are you sure the rink is ready?" she asked nervously as he tugged her toward the door.

He nodded. Micah was absolutely certain the skating arena was prepared for her to practice. He'd had workers there since the day he'd arrived in Amesport. The place was in good-enough shape for them to use, and the ice had been completely repaired so Tessa would be safe. The building might be neglected, but it was sturdy.

He grabbed his own skates from the chair by the door as they exited the front entrance, letting go of her hand as they stepped outside and into the humid, warm air. Fall hadn't yet arrived in Amesport, and the weather was unusually hot, the midday sun out in full force.

He locked the door as Tessa walked to his vehicle, a large black pickup that he'd rented when he'd arrived in Maine.

Tessa didn't speak as they drove the short distance to the arena, which gave Micah more time than he needed to think.

What if she gets hurt?

He grimaced, knowing she'd have to eventually practice some risky moves that could end up with Tessa bleeding and broken on the ice. By education, he was an engineer, and he made his activities as safe as possible. His team was constantly coming up with new safety features for his equipment, which had made him the leader in the industry. Sure, he'd broken a few bones and gotten banged up more times than he could count. There was always an element of risk, certain things beyond his control, but he thrived on the excitement, and he was pretty sure of his engineering skills. His main goal was to keep improving his equipment. People like him were always going to participate in dangerous sports, but he wanted to at least decrease the risk as much as possible.

But it's not about me this time.

It wasn't *him* taking the risk, and *that* scared the hell out of him.

Concern continued to eat at him as he parked the truck and they made their way into the old rink.

Tessa immediately sat down on one of the wooden benches and started to haul on her skates. "I didn't know you could skate," she said, her glance curious now.

He waited until she looked at him again for an answer before replying, "I played a lot of hockey as a teenager and some when I was in college." He didn't have the skills she used to have on ice, or the finesse, but he could hold his own at rough-and-tumble skating.

He put on the skates he'd had his assistant send to him, in a steadily darkening mood, wishing to hell he'd never read Tessa's mail. How *had* his charity found Tessa, anyway? Micah had known about the planned reunion event, but he didn't have a clue how the organizers had tracked down past Olympic athletes. Tessa stayed far away from the media, from what she'd told him, and he doubted the committee had even known she was deaf. They only knew that she had retired, which was the story in the sports world. Nobody knew much more about her sudden retirement, and since it had been years, almost nobody cared.

Honestly, he didn't get that involved in the Sinclair Fund. The organization was large and had employees to deal with the day-to-day business. All of the Sinclairs gave to the Fund, and they recommended it to other businessmen, but none of them was really actively involved. It wasn't possible since they all had busy lives.

"I'm ready," she said stoically as she finished lacing her second skate.

Hastily finishing with his laces, he stood at the same time she did, following her as she stomped toward the ice. She removed the blade guards from her skates and tossed them onto a bench. "I can do this," she whispered quietly.

Micah's heart sank as he watched the indecision and a flash of fear in her expression. He was so damn tempted to just haul her back to the truck and forget about the damn skating.

Her words weren't meant for him; she was trying to reassure *herself.*

That she needed to pep-talk herself onto the ice was reason enough for Micah to call off the whole damn thing. Tessa didn't need to prove herself to anyone.

She stepped onto the ice quickly, so fast that he didn't even have time to talk to her, see if she wanted to just leave. He was guessing she felt that she needed to either make a move or run back to the truck. His heart swelled as he watched her face her fear head-on.

She started slowly, a little unsure during her first rotation around the square arena. He watched her pick up speed with more than a little apprehension, switching directions as she moved.

Forward.

Backward.

Forward.

Backward.

He lost track of time as he stood beside the rink, his grip on the wooden, waist-high wall so strong that the blood was leaving his fingers.

"Christ!" he rasped as he watched Tessa leap into the air in graceful splits. He gulped in a breath, not releasing the air in his lungs until she'd landed safely.

His eyes never left her mesmerizing movements as all thoughts of skating to her rescue left his brain. She didn't need *him.* She'd once been the world's best figure skater, and she was quickly regaining her confidence. Her skills hadn't gone anywhere. They'd just lain dormant until this very moment, and he felt pretty damn lucky just to be an observer.

She moved as if she was going through one of her routines, substituting easier moves for some of the more complicated jumps that had likely been part of her program. Micah caught a glimpse of her face as she sped by him, her skin glowing, her expression euphoric and expressive.

Tessa was born to perform, but the opportunity had been taken away from her too damn soon. She'd told him that she'd been training to do the next Olympics as the defending gold medalist when she'd lost her hearing. Unfortunately, she'd never had that chance to defend her title.

Flowing back into the center of the ice, Tessa literally became a blur of movement as she started to spin faster and faster before finally coming to an abrupt stop, her beautiful body holding a graceful pose for one breathtaking moment before she lowered her arms.

"I did it. I can do it." She was panting as she spoke.

Micah could hear her words from the sideline, and he wondered at the amazement in her voice. Had she been convinced that she *couldn't* skate? A person didn't lose those kinds of skills. Tessa—Theresa Sullivan—had been ice-skating since she could walk, and the training during her adolescence and young adulthood had been intense.

He applauded as Tessa bowed elegantly, but he stopped as she dropped to her knees, her hands over her face.

She's crying.

He jumped onto the ice and breached the distance between them in an instant, dropping down in front of her, completely oblivious to the freezing cold of the ice beneath his knees. "Tessa. What the hell happened?" he asked urgently even though she couldn't hear him, trying to move her hands from her face.

Loud, heart-wrenching sobs filled the air, and Micah felt his heart hammering in alarm. "Are you hurt?"

"No," she wailed, her shoulders rising and falling as she continued to release her emotions. "I did it, Micah. I skated," she answered tearfully, finally removing her hands from her face, resting them on her thighs. "I heard the music in my head. I still remember it."

"Of course you did, sweetheart. You were amazing," Micah told her soothingly, fucking relieved that she wasn't injured.

He was taken aback as she threw herself into his arms with wild abandon and continued to cry.

Recovering quickly, he wrapped his arms around her, sheltering her while years of uncertainty and fear were sobbed out on his shoulder.

Micah shuddered. He might be an asshole, but there was no way he could be unmoved by watching a woman like Tessa cry like years of emotional tension were being expelled from her body, in tears of happiness and incredulous relief.

"Thank you," she choked out between sobs.

He stroked her hair, knowing they were probably the two sweetest words he'd ever heard.

CHAPTER 4

Eventually, Tessa stopped blubbering like an idiot, but she didn't leave the safety of Micah's arms. Her entire body was trembling, and it had been so damn difficult to force herself to get back on the ice. But once there, she'd never felt anything more magical.

Her body had taken over, following the sequence of movements that must have been ingrained in her psyche. It hadn't really been necessary to think much about what she'd been doing. All she'd had to do was listen to the music in her head and skate.

She relaxed against Micah's hard, well-defined body, savoring the feel of his powerful muscles against her softer form. The sense of connection between them made her release a contented sigh. Her world might be silent, but all the rest of her senses were on high alert.

Micah smelled like rough, male temptation, and he felt like sensual sin. What was just a comforting hug to him was something far different for her.

Don't even think about it, Tessa. Micah Sinclair is just a friend.

Finally, she pulled back to look at him. "I think I can do this. I'd need to practice the more complicated jumps, and somehow I need to know I'm matching the music in my head to the recording that's playing, but I don't think it's impossible. I'll just need to make up signals that somebody can give me from the sideline to keep me on track with the music."

He grinned at her, an unruly lock of hair on his forehead making him appear more carefree than she'd seen him since he'd arrived in Amesport. "Almost nothing is impossible," he replied.

"Maybe for you," she answered teasingly.

Some of the things Micah had done in the past just to prove they weren't insurmountable feats made her heart clench. She'd watched the TV breathlessly as Micah and his well-known team of elite skydivers had performed stunts that had never been attempted before, and she'd breathed a sigh of relief as each one of them finally landed on solid ground. In his younger days, it had seemed that his sole objective had been to set world records, and many of them had still never been broken. There weren't many crazy things that hadn't been done in the past by one of the richest and well-known daredevils in the world: Micah Sinclair.

He stood and pulled her up beside him. "Not for you, either," he answered, both signing and speaking so she'd catch his words.

Hell, he even does ASL well. Is there anything he can't do?

Micah had told her about the deaf friend he'd met in college, which was why he knew ASL so well. According to him, he hadn't used the skills in years because his buddy had gotten cochlear implants and didn't use ASL anymore. But he didn't look rusty or hesitant. He signed confidently and with as much cockiness as he did everything else.

She could argue that plenty of things were impossible for her, but she was relieved just to have gotten through the experience of being back on the ice. For so many years, she'd been afraid that she wouldn't be able to skate again. Whether the notion had been rational or not, she'd been too afraid to find out whether or not she'd lost her skills along with her hearing. The two things *were* intertwined: skating and music.

Without being able to hear the notes, she'd assumed that she'd be unable to perform at the same level as before.

I'm out of practice, but I can work up to doing the more difficult jumps.

Tessa had done it once, and she knew she could do it again. Maybe she wouldn't be of the same caliber as before. She was older, deaf, and hadn't worked on any skating routines in years. But the raw ability was still there to be able to perform a good routine. She just needed time on the ice.

Her heart was still pounding with exertion and euphoria as she looked up at Micah and smiled. She was grateful to him for pushing her, making something she loved part of her life again.

The deliciously dangerous, hungry look in his eyes made her smile falter, her body start to clamor for something far more primal than a hug.

I can't want him. He's a Sinclair and I'm a washed-up former Olympic champion. He dates supermodels, for God's sake. I can't confuse his kindness for desire.

Tessa had fought her instincts for days now, and it was getting harder and harder not to remember Micah's hard, muscular body completely nude. God, he'd been breathtakingly perfect, a flawless specimen of masculinity that wouldn't leave her mind. Unfortunately, that image had never gone away, and when he looked at her like he wanted to have *her* for dinner, she was so damn tempted to throw herself at him and beg him to make a meal of her.

She froze, unable to break his gaze, the longing she felt reflected in his gorgeous dark eyes.

He can't want me. He can't want me. He can't want me.

The mantra pounded in her head, but she met him halfway as his head lowered and he captured her mouth with his, blowing the chant straight from her brain.

He *did* want her right now, and she wanted him back.

Tessa moaned as his decadent embrace swept everything from her mind except getting closer, getting more of the sweet, assertive dominance of his mouth. His tongue probed demandingly, as though he wanted to own her. She opened to his commands, happily succumbing to the rampant pleasure that was Micah's domination of her senses.

He was relentless as he freed her hair and sunk his fingers into the curls that sprang from their confinement, tilting her head with her unbound locks so he could plunder deeper.

Yes. Yes. Yes.

Her body sang with sensual longing as she wrapped her arms around his neck, feeling like she wanted to crawl inside him. Her hands speared into his hair, her heart pounding with excitement as the sensation of the coarse tendrils threaded through her fingers. Her world was quiet, which left her so much more focused on the sensations, making them so much more sensually delicious.

Closing her eyes, she allowed both sight and sound to be eliminated, leaving her only the feel of Micah. She let herself drown in his increasingly passionate embrace, her nipples hardening as he jerked her closer, molding her body against his harder form. Her core clenched hard as he put one strong hand on her ass and lifted her up until her pelvis was grinding into him, her legs wrapping around his waist.

He moved on his blades, but she scarcely noticed when he plopped her butt down on the wall of the rink, barely breaking his sensual assault as his lips trailed down the sensitive skin of her neck.

"More, Micah. I need more," she whimpered, fisting his hair in desperation as his mouth left her skin. He pulled her head back to look at him.

Automatically, her eyes opened and she looked at his mouth. "I need to touch you, Tessa. I need to watch you come for me."

The look in his eyes was insistent and feral. "Then touch me," she pleaded. "Please."

She couldn't bear for the intense sensation to be over.

She needed . . .

She burned . . .

She had to have something to stop the fiery ache between her thighs, the painful puckering of her nipples, the fierce longing in her soul.

It had been so long since anyone had touched her intimately, and she'd never been overwhelmed by this kind of passion . . . ever.

The first touch of his fingers on her core wrenched a moan from deep inside her throat. Micah caressed her softly over the fabric of the skimpy material, then delved beneath it, baring her pussy as he shifted the fabric aside.

Tessa shivered as the cold air in the rink wafted between her thighs, the feeling chillingly erotic. Out of habit, she'd waxed, leaving her bare in preparation for wearing a skating skirt again. It left her feeling vulnerable and aroused as Micah stroked over that sensitive naked skin.

Her fingers tightened in his hair, and she tried to close her eyes, but he stopped until she opened them again. "Please." It was the only word she could get out of her mouth. Her brain and body were senseless and greedy, wanting nothing except Micah's hands on her.

"Don't close your eyes," he insisted. "Watch me. Watch who is about to make you come."

Like she could forget? Tessa shuddered when his fingers deftly delved between her saturated folds, the large digits exploring like they wanted every one of her secrets.

"Oh, God," she whimpered, her body responding to every single movement he made.

There wasn't a second of hesitation as he sought and found her clit, rolling over it again and again with his thumb as his fingers explored deeper.

Her breathing became ragged as he thrust a finger into her slick sheath, her muscles contracting around it as though they had a mind of their own.

"Yes. Please, Micah," she cried as her hips moved and tried to grind against his hand.

"I'll take care of you, Tessa," he told her, her eyes still glued to his face. "Christ! You're so tight, but so damn wet for me. You feel so fucking good."

"I want you!" she screamed, almost unable to keep her eyes open and on his face.

"Good. Because I've wanted you ever since I first saw you." His eyes were tumultuous as he drove her higher and higher.

If her mind was functional, she would have doubted his claim, but her body was in control, Micah playing it like a musical instrument that belonged to him.

She fell into the rapid rhythm of Micah retreating and entering her channel while he teased her clit mercilessly with his thumb.

Her belly fluttered and then the knot she'd been feeling there began to unfurl as he moved impossibly faster.

His eyes stayed glued intensely on her face, his expression determined. The carnal, heated look in his eyes made her come undone. Since she couldn't hear, it made his stormy gaze so much hotter. There was only sight and sensation, and both combined were highly erotic.

Her climax washed over her body like waves in a turbulent, stormy sea, sending her body adrift while the pulsations of release seized her, pummeled her.

"Yes. Oh, God." Her eyes closed as she shuddered with the aftermath of her climax.

She was trembling as Micah lowered his mouth and kissed any breath she had left right out of her body. Still, she kissed him back, trying to communicate every emotion she was feeling.

Finally, he wrapped both of his arms around her tightly as she became a panting mess in his embrace.

His unique, masculine scent filled her nostrils as she rested her head against his chest, completely spent. This man had rocked her world, and he hadn't removed a single article of his own clothing.

He pulled her head back gently with her hair. "You looked so beautiful when you were coming, Tessa. You still do."

She shook her head. "I'm a mess," she admitted.

"I want you so damn much. But not here. Not like this." He paused before asking, "Have you been with anyone recently? You're so damn tight."

Tessa wanted Micah so desperately that she considered lying, but she couldn't. She liked him too much, owed him too much to not be honest. "I've haven't been with anybody since I lost my hearing," she confessed. "Before that, there was only one man."

She watched as the expression on his face turned incredulous and then wary.

"That long?" he asked. "How? Why?"

Tessa shook her head. "I was barely twenty-one when I lost my hearing. I was engaged to a man I'd met while I was competing in the Olympics. He was older than me, and an important businessman. I think I was overwhelmed by his attention. Eventually, I figured out that he just wanted a female athlete on his arm for his business and his ego. An Olympic champion. He owns a sports-equipment company, and when I couldn't be that showpiece for him anymore, he dumped me." She paused, remembering how she'd turned herself inside out to be the woman that Rick had wanted her to be, even *before* she'd gone deaf. She'd dressed, walked, and talked just the way he wanted her to, and she'd gone along with it, still amazed that a man as accomplished and wealthy as Richard Barlow wanted her.

In the beginning, Rick had bowled her over, wined and dined her until she was mesmerized by his larger-than-life presence. In the end, she'd found out just what he was really made of—a big pile of crap. Nothing about Rick had been real, and she hadn't been the love of his life. She'd been his slave, molded into the perfect image of what he'd wanted. Unfortunately, the sculpted Theresa Sullivan had fallen apart, and her ex-fiancé hadn't wanted any of part of Tessa. He'd only cared about the exceptional athlete.

His rejection had been a crushing blow to a woman who was still trying to accept the world in a whole new way. She'd moved back to Amesport with her parents and started to build a whole new life again as a deaf woman. But life had delivered several harder blows before she could even begin to cope with becoming deaf and losing the man who had seduced her into her first and only intimate relationship.

She briefly explained her thoughts to Micah, telling him that there hadn't really been a guy who was interested in her since she'd lost her hearing and Rick had broken their engagement.

Really, no guy had ever taken the time to get to know her after she'd become deaf.

"Believe me, they're interested. You're too damn beautiful to pass *any* guy without him wanting you."

Tessa heard his *voice* in her head.

In her mind, Micah was almost growling. The imagined tone was low and savage, matching his savage expression.

It wasn't like she intended to be self-deprecating, but that she was at a disadvantage in the dating world was fact.

She shrugged. "I haven't met any of those men," she answered glumly, knowing that it could possibly be her standoffishness that kept men away. She didn't want to go through the heartache she'd suffered in the past again. Right now, she was safe, and she liked it that way.

"Yes, you have met one," Micah answered, jamming a finger into his chest. "Me. I want you."

Micah was an exception. Tessa knew he wanted her, but she didn't understand why. "You make me feel things I've never felt," she confessed.

Micah could make her body burn with just a glance, like the dangerous look that he was wearing now.

Tessa let him lift her from the wall of the rink, breaking eye contact with him as he lowered her slowly to the ice. He held her hand as she stepped out of the rink and sat down on a bench to remove her skates.

Maybe he was uncomfortable with her confession, but they'd been in the process of becoming friends for the last few days. While she wasn't always as forthcoming as she'd just been because of her past, she didn't lie to friends, either. While it was obvious that Micah was lusting after her, she felt more than just lust.

When they were both ready to leave, Micah reached for her hand, but hesitated before leading her to the door.

"Why is it that you haven't tried cochlear implants? Are you not a candidate?"

Tessa stiffened, pulling her hand from his. "I am. And I tried. It didn't work." He was broaching the last subject she wanted to discuss right now.

"Why?"

She sighed, knowing she wasn't getting away with a partial explanation. "I was thrilled when I had the surgery for the first one and I started to hear again. The voices were kind of robotic and nothing like I remembered, but I got used to it, and the sounds started to sound more normal after a while." She paused, remembering the pain of losing her hearing all over again. "Then I got an infection, and the device started to fail. They had to remove the implant, and I was deaf again before I even had the chance to have the second one done."

Maybe it was better that she'd never had the full experience of hearing again. Maybe it had made the loss easier. But she couldn't help but remember the crushing disappointment of the implant not working. She couldn't imagine anything being much worse.

"Can't you try it again?"

Tessa moved toward the door with Micah right on her tail. "I could, but the risk of infection is still there, and it's expensive. We need the restaurant more than we need me to hear right now."

"Insurance—"

"Doesn't cover everything," she interrupted as she turned and saw the word on his lips. "The implants are outrageous, around a hundred thousand dollars for both sides. Liam and I don't have the kind of money to try again. We'd just be throwing money away if it doesn't work. I want the restaurant restored before I even think about doing the surgery. It's how we make our living. It's our parents' legacy. We can't let it go any longer."

"But if it could give you back your hearing, isn't it worth taking a risk someday?"

"No!" Tessa turned her back on him and pushed her way through the door, leaving Micah behind to lock up the skating rink.

CHAPTER 5

Later that evening, Tessa lay in bed and tried to read, but she was restless. She'd been a real bitch to Micah. After all, he'd just been trying to help. Tessa knew that, but the ache of disappointment over the failure of her attempted implant still haunted her. Insurance did cover a lot, but she knew Liam had shelled out money they didn't have to help her hear again. She'd gotten some offers for endorsements along with her gold medal, but Richard had discouraged her from anything that took away from her skating. He'd said there would be time enough for her to make money later, but that time hadn't ever come. She'd lost the opportunities in order to be Richard's personal star. She regretted so many things she'd done, how she'd handled her post-Olympic years. All of that time, all of those offers wasted on a man who hadn't been worth it.

I was so young and so ignorant.

She sighed as she thought about her failed cochlear implant. She'd had her hearing again, even if things did sound different with the device placement. Her hope had been to get the other ear done and have her life fully restored.

That had never happened.

Instead, she'd been submerged in a soundless world, the same place she'd been living before the implant. Sometimes she was convinced that it was better to never have that experience again, to be satisfied that she was safe and content rather than experience that kind of devastation. She'd plummeted into a depression that had nearly swallowed her whole after the failed implant. It had been the final knockout punch after her parents had died, and it was a place she never wanted to visit again.

Granted, she would probably handle the situation better now. A lot of her heartache was resolved, but there was still a wariness that she couldn't shake, a desire to protect herself from falling down so far she couldn't get up.

Tessa shuddered and tossed her book on the bedside table. Shifting the covers aside, she got up, knowing she wasn't going to sleep anytime soon.

She was already taking a chance by even attempting to perform again. There was every possibility she could fall on her ass and make a fool of herself, but that risk had always been there, even when she'd had her hearing. Tessa knew she could handle that pressure. It was familiar.

The unknown was much scarier.

She felt the rumble in her stomach and realized she was hungry. Not knowing what to do with her restlessness, she stopped in the kitchen and made herself a sandwich. She'd been so thrown off balance by Micah's questions about her implants that she'd sprinted out of his truck when he dropped her off, not asking him in for dinner like she usually would.

Frowning as she scooped tuna into a pita pocket, Tessa admitted that she missed his company, regretted not asking him to have dinner with her. She was getting used to him being around the house, and her heart skittered as she contemplated what had happened at the skating rink. Micah had turned her world upside down so easily, with little more than a kiss and an intimate touch.

I don't regret it, but I can't take this any further with him.

Micah Sinclair was dangerous—a guy she knew she could end up caring about way too much. There was nothing there but heartache for her in her future if she didn't put her walls up with him now. The difficulty was . . . he was simply hard to set boundaries with. He was bossy, but that wasn't why she was struggling to keep him at arm's length.

It's the connection I feel with him.

For some unknown reason, she really didn't have a hard time telling Micah how she felt about anything. Hell, he could make her spill her guts if she wasn't careful. He was just that good at dragging the truth from her, and he did it without being judgmental. Honestly, he was just really easy to talk to. For a man who cheated death for a living, he was incredibly grounded in the real world.

Tessa devoured her sandwich over the sink, smiling at the assortment of chocolate bars she had picked up at the market. Micah ate fairly healthy, but chocolate was his downfall. It was actually one of Tessa's favorite sweets, too, but she stayed away from it since she was back into her conditioning. Nothing packed on the pounds faster than chocolate for her. She might as well take one from the wrapper and apply it onto her ass. That was how fast it would make her gain weight. Since she had spent years avoiding it, she still only indulged on special occasions.

I think tonight is one of those occasions.

Snatching a Snickers bar from the pile on the counter, she was just unwrapping it when she saw her cell phone light up in the dimly lit kitchen. She took a big bite of the chocolate, nut, and caramel mix with a slight moan of pleasure, then unlocked her phone with one finger as it rested beside the sink.

She noticed that she had a message from Micah, and she flipped the text open curiously. They'd exchanged numbers in case they had to cancel a meet up at the rink or for their runs, but had never communicated that way. There had never been a reason.

Micah: I'm hungry. I think you ruined me by making me meals every day.

Tessa snorted, nearly choking on her chocolate. Then she smiled. The complaint was so typical of Micah that it was funny. And she found it amusing that food was the reason he'd contacted her.

Right now, she was relieved that he was trying to breach the gulf that had come between them at the arena earlier in the day.

She typed a quick message back with one finger as she finished the Snickers, tossing the wrapper in the trash under the sink.

Tessa: You have to fend for yourself occasionally. BTW... I'm eating your chocolate.

She knew he was near his phone when he answered immediately.

Micah: It better not be the Snickers. It's my favorite.

She licked her fingers with an evil grin before rinsing and drying them at the sink.

Tessa: It was. It was delicious. My favorite, too.

Micah: I'm confiscating them all tomorrow if you can't control yourself.

She picked up her phone and carried it back to the bedroom, typing a response as she sat cross-legged on the bed.

Tessa: I'm sorry about earlier. I wasn't very nice and I know you were just trying to help.

It took him a few minutes to answer.

Micah: I get it. It was obviously a bad experience.

Of course he understood. He always did. Before she could answer, he sent more.

Micah: Just don't deprive me of the chance for dinner again. I get cranky.

She rolled her eyes.

Tessa: Is that all you ever think about?

Micah: No. When I'm around you I think about banging you most of the time.

His reply was blunt, but she laughed anyway.

Tessa: That can't happen again.

Micah: Ok. I'd rather use my mouth anyway.

She sucked in a breath, the image of Micah's head between her thighs enough to make her squirm.

Tessa: That's not what I meant. I was trying to say we can't be intimate in any way. I don't do casual sex. What happened was amazing, and I got caught up in the moment. It was an emotional day. But I don't think I'd like myself very much if something else happened.

Micah: I'd make sure you loved it.

She sighed, wondering if she could have a fling with him. Maybe it would never go anywhere, but she needed to sate the aching need she had for him to bury himself inside her, for him to claim her body. She tried to reason with him again.

Tessa: I don't do casual sex.

Micah: Sex with you would never be casual.

She knew what he meant. Even if something happened, it would never just be a screw for her.

Tessa: What would it be?

Micah: Intense.

His one-word answer made her heart flutter. She knew he was right.

Tessa: Why do you even want me? No other single woman on Earth would turn you down.

He was smart, insanely gorgeous, and a billionaire Sinclair. She was pretty sure women were practically throwing themselves at him.

Micah: I don't want anyone else. I want you.

Her breath caught, her body on fire and Micah wasn't even physically near her.

Tessa: You can't have me. I can't do it. I'm sorry.

Even as she sent the message, she knew her body wouldn't be able to resist him if he pushed. *Please, please. For once . . . don't push.*

Micah: Friends?

She wasn't sure whether to be relieved or saddened by his question.

Tessa: Yes.

Micah: I don't think I've ever had a female friend.

Tessa: Stop dating supermodels and maybe you wouldn't feel the need to do them all.

Micah: I don't really date. Haven't for a long time.

Tessa: You're always being pictured with beautiful women.

Micah: Acquaintances who want to go to a party or event. I don't fuck them.

Tessa: You don't?

Micah: Nope. You jealous?

She stopped to think before answering.

Tessa: I have no right to be jealous. I'm just a friend.

Micah: You're not just a friend, Tessa. But if that's what you want, I'll do my best to be that for you.

She knew she would never regard him as just a friend after the intimate moments they'd had together that afternoon, even though that's exactly how it needed to be.

Tessa: I'm going to bed now.

She needed to stop the conversation before she begged him to come over and fuck her up against the wall or over the table. Anything to stop the frustrated desire pounding at her right now.

Micah: Wish I was going with you. I'll see you in the morning. Dream about me.

She chuckled at his arrogance as she put the phone on the table beside her discarded book and flopped back onto the pillow, then tugged the cord on the bedside lamp to shut off the light.

Tessa had a hard time falling asleep, and when she did, Micah got his wish.

Her dreams were vivid and erotic.

Carnal.

Breathtaking.

And every one of her dreams featured Micah Sinclair as the man who broke through her outer shell of fear and forced her to yield to their passion.

Dammit!

CHAPTER 6

"So what's the deal with your ex-fiancé?" Micah asked right before he took a huge slug of water.

Tessa tensed. She and Micah had taken a different route on their run today, a path through the woods that had ended in a clearing by the ocean. He'd wanted to stop since the route had been longer than their usual run. Her eyes were drawn to him, his head turned toward her as he stretched out on the grass beneath them, a ragged T-shirt clinging to his damp, powerful chest and muscular biceps.

"What do you mean? He was my fiancé, and then we broke up," she replied uncomfortably. She didn't like to talk about Rick to anyone. He was history, a part of her life that she didn't want to discuss.

"Why?" he asked casually.

Tessa messed with her hair, re-securing it after some of her curls had come loose during her run. Micah irked her when he got this insistent. He was obviously going to wring the answer from her, no matter how long it took. She was looking at his face now, and she recognized his determined expression.

She sighed as she let her hands drop, her hair confined once more. "Do you really want to know?" she asked warily, hoping he'd say he didn't, but knowing it wasn't going to happen.

"Yes."

That's what I was afraid of!

He leaned back and propped himself up on his arms, still staring at her expectantly.

God, he looked good. The morning light reflected from his hair, the mild wind ruffling it just enough for him to look sexy. Her eyes trailed down to his sweatpants and expensive running shoes. How did a woman tell a man who looked like him about being dumped?

"He was a rich and powerful man. We were together from the time I turned eighteen, right after the Olympics. He talked me into going back to Boston with him after we'd dated for a few months. I did. We lived together for a year before he asked me to marry him." She stopped, thinking about how naive she had been back then. She'd thought she was living her dream, that she'd found the one man who would love her forever. Life was never that simple, and her relationship with Rick had become incredibly demanding and complicated.

"And?" Micah prompted.

"Back then, I guess I thought our life was good. I traveled with him when I could. It worked out well because my coach was in Boston, so she could go back home after we moved in together. I went to his parties, became the woman he wanted."

He looked at her sharply. "What does that mean?"

"He didn't approve of the clothing I wore, some of my habits, my friends. I turned myself inside out to change. He needed a woman who was more mature."

"You were fucking eighteen years old, and had spent your entire life devoted to your sport. How much more did he want?" Micah asked, his expression dark.

"Everything," Tessa admitted. "He wanted me dressed differently, my behavior more proper and sophisticated. He wanted me to cultivate friends in his circle."

Micah shook his head. "Snobs."

She shrugged. "Pretty much. I realized later how much I hated that life no matter how many fancy parties and events we attended. It wasn't me. I was still a small-town girl. I didn't belong there."

"You didn't belong with *him*. How did you break up?"

"After I lost my hearing and left the hospital, things were never the same. I learned how to read lips as fast as I could, but he hated the fact that I was deaf. I was handicapped, and he hated to take me anywhere." More quietly she whispered, "He was ashamed of me, I think. He got involved with another woman, and broke off our engagement on his birthday. He asked me to get out the next day. I guess he had my replacement ready to move in."

"What an asshole. Who is he?" His expression was dangerous now.

"Richard Barlow. A multimillionaire who attends a lot of sporting events."

"I've met him. He's a pretentious prick. We've run into each other a few times. Since we're both in the sports-equipment business, we cross paths, even though my company specializes in extreme sports."

Moving closer, Tessa put a hand on his forearm. "It doesn't matter anymore. I made a lucky escape. If I had married him, I doubt I'd be the same person I am right now."

"Yes, you would. But you'd also be his puppet on the outside, and that would have made you miserable. You shouldn't have to change for anybody. You're fucking perfect just the way you are." He looked angry.

She decided to finish the story she'd started. "I came back home and started helping Mom and Dad run the restaurant. Liam was gone then, so it was just us. My brother came home for good when Dad died. He's been here ever since. He gave up his job as a special-effects expert in movies and TV to be here for me."

"Which is why you have a hard time telling him to mind his own business," Micah concluded.

"Yes. I know he means well, but I don't need his help anymore. I'm grateful that he was there when I needed him, but he doesn't have to keep sacrificing now. The only thing I need is his love. But I don't think he's realized that yet. I want him to move on with his life because I'm moving on with mine. But he still blames himself for my hearing loss."

"What happened?" Micah asked, his expression less irate.

Tessa sighed and lay back on the soft grass. "Nothing that was in any way his fault. We were both busy, but we wanted to get together. Meeting here in Amesport was the easiest for both of us, because Liam and I both loved to be outside. One of our favorite things to do together was hiking. I got here before he did, and he had to bail on our hiking trip. He got tied up on a job and couldn't make it back to Maine. I decided to go to one of our favorite areas and do the hike by myself. It was only one day, and it wasn't like I hadn't done it before." She rolled and propped her head on her hand, facing Micah.

"You got hurt while you were out hiking?"

She shook her head. "Not hurt. Sick. I wasn't feeling that great when I started out in the morning, but I thought it was stress. I'd been out of the country for competitions, and my travel schedule was crazy. I'd just gotten back in the States, and I flew here to Maine directly from a competition. I was tired, but as I got farther and farther along on the hike, I guess I spiked a fever. I got turned around, and eventually I was way off the hiking trail. Honestly, I don't remember much of the whole hiking ordeal."

"Then what?"

Tessa could tell from the look on Micah's face that he was listening intently, his body tensed. Her world might be silent, but she'd become a master at reading expressions and body language.

She shrugged. "All I remember is being tired and cold. I sat down to rest, and that's about the only memory I have of getting sick. I don't recall being alone that night. They didn't find me until the next afternoon. My parents got worried and called Liam. Then my brother notified the authorities. Everything is a blank until I woke up in the hospital, terrified because I couldn't hear a thing that anybody was saying. I had bacterial meningitis. Liam filled in some of the blanks, but it's like I lost that whole week of my life before I woke up. Then when I finally opened my eyes, I was deaf."

Micah flopped down on his stomach next to her, his eyes softening as he reached for her hand. "You must have been scared."

Tessa savored the feel of their palms meeting, Micah's larger hand engulfing hers. "I was terrified," she admitted. "When I was well enough, I communicated in writing, but it was frustrating."

"So Liam blames himself because he wasn't there with you," Micah guessed.

"He does. He said if he had been there, I could have gotten help a lot faster, and I might not have lost my hearing."

"Is that true?"

"Who knows? But I'm the one who decided to go alone, and all my parents knew was that I was going hiking. They didn't really worry until the next morning. Nobody knew I was going to get sick while I was out in the woods, or that it would be that serious. You don't think about those kinds of things, especially at that age. It happened so fast."

Tessa saw his reproving look before he spoke. "You could have died out there."

"But I didn't. I'm grateful that I didn't. But Liam thinks he's entirely responsible for ruining my life and my career. It's ridiculous. He had nothing to do with my decision. I was an adult. Sometimes I think I was born all grown up." She'd never had time to play as a child and teen. Her life back then had been filled with nothing but practice routines and competitions.

He grinned at her, a wolfish smile that made her heart clench. "Maybe you need to play."

Tessa rolled her eyes. "I'm a little too old for that."

"You're never too old to play."

"Says the perpetual boy who does nothing but crazy things that most adults wouldn't even consider doing."

Micah's expression grew troubled as he answered, "Not as much as I'd like to anymore. I have a company to run and a family to watch out for now. The only sport I focus on now is my skydiving team, for the most part."

"No parents?" Tessa asked curiously.

He looked somber as he said, "Not anymore. They died a year ago."

Tessa took her hand from his and put a palm lightly on his face. "I'm sorry. How did it happen?"

"My dad retired early, moved to California with Mom to avoid the cold winters. There was a home-invasion robbery. My parents were both murdered. Xander was the only one there with them, and the only one who survived . . . if you want to call it survival. He was able to reach for his cell phone and call the police. There was a shootout with the murderer a few miles from my parents' home. The guy who killed our parents died, too, but I don't think it made any of us feel better."

Tessa's eyes watered, her heart aching for Micah. She had lost her own parents, and she knew the pain of losing both of the people she loved most in the world relatively close together. But the shock of losing both of his parents at the same time to murder had to have been devastating. "What do you mean? Your brother did make it, right?"

"He's alive, if that's what you mean. But he's never been the same man. He was an incredibly talented musician, and he was world famous. Unfortunately, he gave up his career. He still hasn't recovered. His physical wounds healed, but he's scarred and messed up emotionally. Drugs, alcohol, and severe depression. I get to the West Coast as much as I can to see him. Not that he *wants* to see *anybody*, but someone needs to keep an eye on him. Right now, I'm not sure whether he cares if he lives or dies."

"I'm so sorry," Tessa replied, a lone tear trickling down her cheek. "For what?"

She rested her hand back in his and squeezed. "Because you've had to be the strong one, the person who took over when your parents died. I'm sorry for your brother, that he had to see your parents die. Was he badly injured?"

"Pretty bad. Both of my parents were shot multiple times, but Xander was shot once, then cut up, stab wounds everywhere. He was in the hospital for a long time. We weren't sure he was going to make it."

Tessa had met Julian briefly when he'd been in Amesport. Xander had never made the trip for any of his cousins' weddings or events, except Sarah and Dante's ceremony, nuptials that Tessa hadn't attended. But she remembered hearing about how handsome all of the Sinclair men had been together in a group. Xander had never come to Amesport again. Now she knew why. "What about Julian?"

"He's living his dream right now. He worked so damn hard to make it in the movie industry. After he got the Academy Award for his first movie, he's been in high demand. He's just wrapping up his third film."

Tessa could tell that Micah was proud of Julian, but was it fair that he wasn't really sharing with Micah the burden of Xander's problems? "But surely Julian could help. You have a business to run, obligations of your own."

Micah shook his head. "He's on location most of the time."

"You don't want Julian to know how bad Xander is doing," Tessa concluded, frowning at Micah. He couldn't keep shouldering all the burdens he was carrying. His obligations to his company had to be demanding. Then, he was traveling from coast to coast for his younger brother? He may have stopped some of his personal participation in extreme sports, but he still had duties as the leader of a very elite skydiving team, Xtreme Dive Crew. Even if a person wasn't into skydiving, there were very few who hadn't heard of Micah's troop of professionals, or seen them perform some crazy dangerous maneuvers. The group was the best of the best, and Micah sponsored and led the team. They were named after his own company, Xtreme Dive Sports Equipment.

"Julian would give up his career if he knew, or severely limit it, to help with Xander. My youngest brother already threw his career as a musician away. I don't want that for Julian." His jaw was firmly set, his eyes shuttered.

A memory flitted through Tessa's mind. "You said Xander was a musician. Was he a rock star?"

Micah looked at her curiously, raising a brow. "Yeah. He *was*. Were you into his music? He started pretty young, probably before you lost your hearing."

Tessa shook her head. "What does he look like?" There were definitely coincidences, but *her* Xander, a kind man she'd never forgotten, and Micah's younger brother couldn't possibly be the same person. What were the chances of that?

"Dark hair. Brown eyes. He just turned thirty."

Tessa quickly thought about his age and description, realizing that they were definitely talking about the same guy. How many successful rockers named Xander could there be in the world?

Her heart ached as she explained, "I met him. Years ago when I lived in Boston. He was doing a concert there. He helped me. I only met him once, but I never forgot how much his assistance meant to me."

Tessa quickly recounted how she and Xander had become acquainted, unable to imagine Micah's younger brother as anything other than how he'd been with her . . . an adorable, cheeky rock star.

"Sounds like something he'd do," Micah agreed. "He's . . . different now."

She couldn't help but be sad about such a nice guy having something so terrible happen to him. Life was so damn unfair sometimes. "Maybe it will just take some time," she suggested, her heart squeezing like it was being clenched by a merciless fist.

"He's not getting better." There was sadness and frustration in Micah's expression.

"He will," Tessa told him, leaning her forehead against his. "I wish there was something I could do to help."

Micah was assisting her right now in so many ways, and she wanted to give him something back. It was obvious that the devastating events that had occurred were getting to him. He'd lost his parents, and now he felt like he was losing his brother.

She squealed with surprise as he sat up and hefted her onto his lap. "You can. Give me your opinion. What do you think of me building my house right here?"

Tessa barely caught his words as she wrapped her arms around his neck, trying to steady herself. "Here?"

She sensed that Micah didn't want to talk about Xander anymore, and Tessa let the subject go. He'd come here to escape for a while, and he deserved a chance to relax and forget about his troubles right now.

"Yep. I think this is a perfect place for a second home." He tightened his arms around her.

"It's beautiful here. Peaceful." As she looked around, all she could see were trees and the massive coastline beyond. It was slightly elevated where they were sitting, so the views would be amazing.

"I thought so, too."

"But I didn't know you wanted to spend more time in Amesport. It's a little tame."

Micah lived for action, for new adventures. Amesport was fun in the summer because of the ocean and the tourists, but she was pretty sure he'd quickly get bored. It certainly wasn't New York City.

"I want to build a home for both of my brothers, too. I want what Jared has: all of his family back together again. I won't live here all the time, but I kind of like the idea of building us homes here like Jared did."

Tessa caught a sense of longing she couldn't explain in his sad smile. "So you bought up all the land on this side of town just to build a few houses."

He shrugged. "It's not like I can't afford it. So yeah, I guess I did."

"And the skating rink?"

"We Sinclairs like our space and our privacy," he answered with a more genuine grin. "I bought the skating arena for the property it sits on, but if you think you'll use it, I'll reopen it."

Tessa looked into Micah's eyes, realizing he was serious. He'd reopen the ice-skating venue just to make her happy. "I'd love to see it open, but I'm not sure how much revenue it would bring. My dad never made much of a profit. It's outside of town, and the tourists come for the coastline and the ocean in the summer. It was mostly locals."

"Then I guess it needs to become the happening place in Amesport. Besides, I don't need to make more money. I'd do it for you."

Tessa's heart did backflips as Micah moved closer, his stare becoming more intense.

"Why? You hardly know me," she asked, perplexed.

Tessa squeaked as her back hit the grass again and Micah pinned her arms beside her head as he answered, "I know you, Tessa. I fucking feel you every single day. I can't be in your company without getting a raging hard-on, and it's driving me half-insane."

His fierce expression made her heart pound hard against her ribs, so hard she could feel it *thumping* inside her chest. Micah's body was resting on top of hers, his weight keeping her plastered against the ground. Her breath hitched as she answered slowly, "I don't understand."

"Then let me be blunt. I want to fuck you so damn badly that I can hardly draw a breath. I want to be buried so deep inside you that you lose yourself completely, and all you want is for me to fuck you hard and fast until you scream my name while you come."

The hunger on his face was visible, and Tessa knew he wasn't lying. Right now, he looked like he was a predator ready to consume her, and heat flooded between her thighs as she conjured up the image he was describing.

Both of us naked, our bodies entwined. Me, losing control while he pumps into my body until I'm screaming, helpless to do anything but climax.

Her belly tightened and her core squeezed so hard with desire that her entire body was shaking.

This is what it's like for a man to really desire me.

It was terrifying and exhilarating at the same time, probably because she wanted him, too.

His face was close, so close she could feel his heated breath against her cheek. Temptation beckoned, the deep longing to feel the ultimate human connection with this man. Him. Micah Sinclair. The only man who'd ever made her tremble with a single touch.

"I can't," she whispered anxiously.

"Can't or won't?" His expression was anguished now.

"Both," she answered vaguely.

There was nothing she wanted more than Micah. Her soul and body were begging her to give in, let herself wallow in the pleasure she knew he could show her, but her rational mind resisted. *Hard.*

And then, he kissed her, his mouth diving for hers like he couldn't stop himself. She relaxed for an instant, let herself follow where his dominant passion led. He cajoled, he teased, and he conquered. She opened for him, letting his tongue roam through her mouth like he owned it. Moaning as she allowed her mouth to meld with his, Tessa realized she was already drowning in sensation and Micah's bold, commanding touch.

Just like I did at the skating arena.

She wanted to let herself go.

She wanted to fall into him and forget.

She desperately wanted the connection she had with him to grow deeper and deeper, until she didn't know her own name.

But she couldn't.

Turning her head, she separated her mouth from his and cried out, "No! I can't. Please. I can't do this again."

He backed off immediately. "What's wrong? Do what again?"

She caught the words on his lips, and she knew she had confused him. Maybe she'd given him the wrong signals when she'd let herself be swept away at the skating rink. She didn't regret it, but she knew it couldn't happen again.

Releasing her wrists, he quickly sat up and pulled her into his lap.

She turned her head and didn't look at him until he forced her chin up with his fingers. "Tell me."

Maybe he deserved an explanation, but she wasn't sure what to say. She ended up blurting out exactly how she felt. "After I broke up with Rick, and my parents died, I went into a horrible depression. I'd lost my hearing, and that had taken away the man I loved. My career was gone, so I was just floating in limbo, everything I cared about gone. I'd completely changed to be the woman Rick wanted, and then I . . . wasn't. My parents were gone, and I was all alone." She stopped briefly to gather her turbulent thoughts, realizing she wasn't making any sense. "He's the only man I ever wanted, but he didn't want me anymore, even though I did everything in my power to please him. In the end, it didn't matter. He dumped me anyway when I wasn't the perfect doll he'd turned me into, going to parties I didn't care about, dressing the way he wanted, acting the way he wanted. None of that mattered anymore because I wasn't the woman he wanted."

"He wasn't the man for you," Micah interjected while Tessa took a steadying breath.

"No. He wasn't. But I didn't know that back then. I was young, and I *let* him become my whole world. He reinvented me because I was young, stupid, and I hadn't completely found myself. Skating was my life. There was nothing else for me until I met Rick. I was too naive not to be programmed to make him happy. And it was nearly my downfall."

She took a deep breath before moving her eyes to his and told him honestly, "I was so depressed that I tried to kill myself. I didn't care whether I lived or died at that point in my life. That's probably what your brother is facing now, except I wasn't drinking or doing drugs every day."

She waited with a heavy heart, knowing he'd look at her differently now, and she knew that rejection from Micah was going to hurt.

It took Micah a few moments to process exactly what Tessa had confessed. Once, she'd been so alone and so desperately lost that she'd wanted to take her life?

He knew he should immediately discard the thought that she would have followed through. She loved her brother, and, deep down inside, the will to survive would never have let her take her own life. Still, the thought of the world with no Tessa scared the shit out of him.

His rage at all of the tragedy that this one small woman had lived through pounded at him relentlessly, making him incapable of saying much of anything.

Finally, he asked, "Have you ever thought about it again?"

She shook her head. "No. I went to counseling. It took me a while to resolve my issues, to really grieve for everything I'd lost. That was a turning point for me. Everything happened so fast that I never really had a chance to mourn. I guess everything stayed bottled up until I finally cracked."

Micah stood, unable to find the words to say, unable to comfort her. He was too busy being angry at the world, pissed off that Tessa had needed to endure so damn much that it nearly broke her.

Nearly. But it hadn't.

He stood and held out his hand to her, then pulled her to her feet. "Everything better now?"

It was a dumb, awkward, almost polite question, but he had to ask.

She nodded. "Better," she agreed. "I'm still working on awesome."

Micah didn't talk much as they made their way back through the woods, lost in his own thoughts. He wished he knew how to comfort Tessa, but he wasn't sure how.

One thing he knew for sure, he damn well was going to get her to "awesome" as soon as he possibly could. She'd had enough shit in her life. It was beyond time for her to become "breathtakingly amazing."

CHAPTER 7

The last thing Kristin Moore wanted to see today was Julian Sinclair walking into Shamrock's Pub. It had already been a shitty day, and seeing Julian come through the door made it an explosive-diarrhea kind of afternoon.

Her parents' bar and grill was between the lunch and dinner rush, and even though it was a Saturday, there was only one couple at the far table having a drink. The tourist season was over, and there wasn't much happening before seven or eight o'clock these days once the lunch crowd had departed.

Of course, Julian swaggered straight to the bar where she was wiping down counters, and plopped his tight, gorgeous ass down on a barstool. "How are you, Red?"

His tone was taunting, like he was already ready for a fight. "Fine, until you got here," she retorted, her teeth set on edge.

What was it about Julian Sinclair that put her immediately on the defensive? In addition to the fact that he was one of the most perfectly gorgeous men she'd ever met, he was a superstar and a billionaire. His platinum-blond hair and deep-blue eyes would turn any woman's head. His perfectly toned body, complete with bulging biceps, would make them do a double take and keep right on staring. He looked the part of a Hollywood A-lister.

He was an amazingly generous tipper, something she'd found out the night of Hope Sinclair's winter ball, when he'd left her a wad of hundred-dollar bills that had helped her make her rent and pay some bills that month.

Unfortunately, he *still* irritated the hell out her.

"Nice greeting. I thought this was a tourist town," Julian said drily.

"The tourists are gone for the season. So what do you want? You're slumming it pretty far from Hollywood, aren't you, Hotshot?"

"Can I just get a beer?" he asked in a less sarcastic tone.

Kristin's gaze inspected his face carefully for the first time since he'd walked in. She'd gotten distracted by his perfectly toned body as he'd come in and sat down.

Now that she had a chance to see him clearly, he looked worn out, and he had some obvious lacerations on that perfect face and a few on his neck. Julian was dressed casually in jeans and a deep-blue polo shirt that matched his eyes, but Kristin couldn't help but notice that he might be just a little bit leaner than he had been the last time she saw him. Granted, he was still gorgeous, but a little worse for wear.

She turned silently and went to the service area in the back of the bar, returning a few minutes later to place a well-loaded fish sandwich in front of him, along with a glass of milk.

"I asked for a beer," he said irritably.

She nodded at the sandwich. "I think you need that more. What happened to you?"

"Action movie," he answered as though those two words explained everything.

"Looks like you got in the middle of the action and came out the loser," she shot back, wanting to smile as he picked up half of the grinder she'd put together and started to eat.

"I didn't lose. We were out in the damn wilderness and I was trying to do as many of the stunts as possible on my own. I got a little banged up." He took another bite and swallowed before adding, "I guess I was hungry. This is good. Is it poisoned?" He didn't seem concerned, because he continued to devour the meal, washing it down with large gulps of the milk.

"I guess you'll find out in about ten minutes," Kristin answered cheerfully. "The toxin is pretty fast acting, Hotshot."

He grinned at her, never slowing down as he finished off his dinner. "You wouldn't bump me off. You like arguing with me too much, Red."

God, she hated that nickname. Her flame-red hair and her rounded body had been her two most hated body traits in her teen years, and she'd had guys call her that a lot back then. It didn't exactly bring back fond memories, and Julian had used that name from the time he'd met her, which had probably put her on the defensive with him almost immediately.

Kristin felt her heart skitter, that stupid smile of his getting to her. "Maybe I'm tired of fighting with you."

"Nope. I don't buy that. You like it," Julian answered right before he took the last bite of his sandwich.

Kristin turned and cut Julian a piece of pie, setting it carefully on a small plate before grabbing a spoon and putting it all in front of him.

"I don't like arguing," she told him honestly. "I just can't seem to help myself."

Insults sprang from her lips so easily when she was in Julian's company. Usually, she didn't have a hair-trigger temper, even though she *was* a redhead, but he seemed to bring out the worst in her.

"How do you know I like chocolate? I could be allergic," Julian purred huskily.

Kristin had given him a piece of the daily special. It was a creamy milk-chocolate pie with whipped cream on the top. She hadn't really had much choice. They only had one kind of pie. "Maybe I was hopeful. Are you allergic?"

"No." Julian picked up the fork and dug into the pie.

"Too bad. Maybe you just look like the kind of guy who gives in to temptation . . . often," Kristin snapped.

Julian looked up from his plate and pinned her with an unnerving stare. "I don't."

The words were hoarse and genuine, which confused Kristin enough to look away from his hypnotic gaze. It was about the only plain speaking he'd ever done in her company, and she shuddered, knowing that those two words were meant as so much more than just a denial. He was trying to tell her something.

"So what *are* you doing here?" she asked in a rush, eager to change the subject.

"The movie just wrapped. I was looking for Micah. His employees said he was here."

Moving a short distance away from Julian, Kristin put her elbows on the bar. Her feet were killing her, and she knew she looked disheveled. Her hair was starting to come loose from the hurried French braid she'd done earlier that morning, and the white apron she was wearing had splatters of food decorating the front from lunch service. "I haven't seen him. I didn't even know he was here."

"He's here. He's staying on the Peninsula in Jared's guesthouse. But I checked. He's not there. Jared said to try Randi's old place. I guess Micah bought some land out there, along with Randi's old house."

Kristin was surprised, and very little shocked her. "He bought an old house outside town? Why?"

"He bought a bunch of property. Some of it's on the coastline. He told Jared it's an investment."

"Why here?" Kristin was still baffled about why some guy with almost unlimited amounts of money would want to buy property in Amesport.

Julian shrugged his broad shoulders. "Why not? He could build up the land, expand the economy in town. I guess I get his plan. But he's not usually a real-estate investor. I think he might have other motives."

Kristin didn't like Julian's evil grin one bit, and she hated the thought of Amesport becoming a completely commercial town. The area had built up over the years, but Amesport still had a small-town feel, and she liked it that way. "What kind of motives?"

Julian pushed his empty plate away and polished off his milk. "Just a hunch. I'll find out if I'm right eventually."

Kristin glared at him. "So you're not sharing?"

"Red, if I'd known you wanted to share, I'd have saved you some of that pie."

He was deliberately misunderstanding her, goading her now. He obviously wasn't going to spill any information. "If you think he's out at Randi's old place, why did you stop here?"

Julian stood up and pulled out a wad of money from the pocket of his jeans and dropped it beside his empty pie plate. "I thought I wanted a beer," he said vaguely.

"Do you still want it?" Kristin tried to ask politely. After all, he was a paying customer.

"Nope." He moved lightning fast and grasped her braid before she could back away from the bar. "I think you gave me what I really needed, Red." He'd moved in quickly, his warm breath tickling her ear. "I only want one more thing."

Kristin felt her body react to his nearness, and it made her almost speechless. "What?" She hated herself because the word came out sounding breathless.

"More dessert," he whispered huskily, tilting her head with her braid as his lips covered hers.

Kristin was startled for a fraction of a second before her entire body began to ignite. She wrapped her arms around Julian's muscular shoulders, trying to tug him closer, desperate for body contact.

The embrace only lasted for a short time, but it was enough to shake Kristin to her core. Julian wasn't shy, and he openly devoured her as the couple in the corner watched curiously.

As he raised his mouth, Kristin opened her eyes, not sure when she'd closed them to savor the moment.

He tucked a stray lock of hair behind her ear, then ran the back of his hand down her cheek. "I won't say I'm satisfied," he rasped. "But I got what I came for."

She came out of her daze as he released her.

What? What had he come for? For a beer? To kiss me senseless? To fill his empty stomach? What?

Kristin never got to ask. Julian departed as quickly as he'd entered, leaving her with only a glimpse of his completely edible body as he walked out the door.

❧

Julian finally got his beer as he sat in the living room of Dante's house, shooting the breeze with his male cousins and his oldest brother, Micah. Evan was the only one missing, still off on his delayed honeymoon with Randi.

"You look like hell," Micah mentioned casually from his seat in the chair next to him.

"Thanks, bro. Nice to see you, too." It wasn't like Julian didn't know he'd lost some weight while he was in the Australian outback filming, but he was sick as hell of being reminded he had a few bruises and scrapes. They'd heal, and he wasn't as worried as his agent that his perfect face would have a scar. *Jesus!* He was tired of everybody worrying about how he looked.

"I'm glad to see you, but it looks like it was a rough job," Micah answered frankly.

"It was." He didn't want to dwell on his latest project. It was a high-profile movie, hyped and anticipated, but for Julian, it hadn't been that much of a challenge other than performing some of the stunts. Honestly, he missed the much rawer film that had won him the Oscar. The current movie he'd just wrapped would be a blockbuster because of the special effects, but it didn't have a whole lot of substance.

"What made you stop here before heading back to California?" Micah asked curiously.

"I'm not sure. I guess I wanted to see what you were up to. When I found out you were here, I thought I'd take a break. It's peaceful." He was bullshitting himself and Micah. Amesport was fairly quiet once the tourists were gone, but it was far from relaxing with Red living here.

"I thought maybe you wanted a ride," Micah said wryly.

"Got my own jet now," Julian shot back at his older brother with humor in his voice after a few chugs from his beer.

"About time," Micah grumbled, taking a pull from his own bottle.

"So what are you doing with the property you bought, Micah?" Grady asked from his seat on the couch. "Hopefully not a subdivision."

Julian looked at Grady's unhappy face, knowing he was possessive about two things: his wife, Emily, and the town of Amesport. Grady had been living here much longer than his brothers, and he liked the seclusion of the Peninsula and the town of Amesport in general.

Micah held up a hand defensively. "I'm not building it up. I'm building a house for myself on the coast, and vacation homes for Julian and Xander. I want to open the old skating rink, too, since I have the property."

"What for?" Dante asked curiously. "It didn't do much when it was open, from what I understand."

Julian looked at his brother and smirked. It was kind of fun to watch Micah squirm.

Micah shrugged. "It's still viable, and it gives the locals something else to do."

Julian wanted to call *bullshit* on his brother, but he didn't.

"You're building for yourself?" Jared asked, sounding astonished. "Damn. It would be great to see you guys around, even if it was only for a vacation."

Jared had always been the *fixer* among the Sinclairs, the one who valued family. He'd done much the same thing as Micah was doing now in order to get him and his family all together again.

And he'd finally succeeded. Jared and all his siblings now resided full-time on the Amesport Peninsula.

Julian eyed Micah suspiciously, wondering if he was hoping for the same result. If so, he was going to be disappointed. Julian and Xander belonged in California, and Micah had his entire company based out of New York. Besides, none of them were exactly lonely. They all had scores of women vying for their attention.

Just not the right one.

The nagging thought crossed through his mind involuntarily, but Julian ignored it. He'd worked his entire life to get where he was in Hollywood, and there was no way he was leaving. He didn't need a vacation house in some small town in Maine. Hell, the winters were frigid, and the temperature wasn't exactly scorching even in the summer, most of the time. Okay, yeah, maybe it would be nice to see his brothers and cousins more, and maybe he'd do a vacation here once in a while. But that was it.

Sometimes he missed his family, but he had a damn cell phone.

Julian continued to listen as Dante, Jared, and Grady all talked about houses, sounding plenty enthusiastic about the prospect of having their cousins owning homes in Amesport.

He downed the rest of his beer, trying not to think about his earlier encounter with Red. If he gave it much thought, he'd end up sporting the same boner he'd had the second he'd seen her again.

She'd surprised him today by quietly giving him dinner and a glass of milk instead of the beer he'd ordered. Strangely, she'd seemed to sense he'd been hungry, tired, and restless, even if she was contrary almost all of the time.

I'm not exactly nice to her.

Nope. He wasn't, and he generally wasn't an asshole. Not really. But something about her made him want to antagonize her.

Because I like her.

Shit! He wasn't in grade school anymore, but damned if he didn't want to tug on her braid because he liked her. He also wanted to see her flushed, her sultry, dark-green eyes flashing fire at him.

Problem was, he wasn't about to bang one of the women here. If his cousins or Micah found out, they'd beat the crap out of him. Kristin was friends with every Sinclair wife, and Hope, his only female cousin. She worked for Dante's physician wife as a medical assistant in her office. Kristin was trouble, and he needed to stay as far away from her as he could get.

The difficulty was, he *wanted* to seek her out.

He tried not to groan as he thought about how passionately she'd returned his kiss today. He hadn't meant for that to happen, but now that it had, the memory wouldn't leave his brain.

"You ready?" Micah asked as he stood.

Julian looked up at his brother questioningly, wondering what he'd missed while he'd been reliving his heated encounter with Kristin. "Yeah. Yeah, I'm ready." He stood up, handing Dante his empty bottle as his cousin collected trash. Once a Los Angeles detective, his cousin looked so domesticated; Dante was still a detective, but now he worked for the police department in Amesport.

He looks happy. Everyone looks so damn happy.

Julian felt a twinge in his chest as he looked at all of his cousins, every one of them appearing like they had everything they wanted in life. Maybe he wasn't the type of man to settle down, his life too mobile and crazy to ever consider a relationship, but at that moment, he almost envied them. Most of the time, he was secretly happy for all his cousins.

They'd lived through a fucked-up childhood. They deserved to be content as adults.

Another sharp pang stabbed him in the chest as the backslapping and jokes started again as he and Micah went to leave, making him remember the times when all of the Sinclair men had spent summers together when they were younger. There was something to be said about always knowing another Sinclair had your back. In California, Julian could rarely tell enemy from friend in his superficial world.

As he followed Micah out the door, Julian wondered if he'd forgotten what it was like to have *anybody* he trusted in his life. Sadly, as he walked away from the comfortable atmosphere of family, he couldn't think of a single person in California who would be at his back if he wasn't a billionaire or his career wasn't going as well as it was right now.

CHAPTER 8

The next afternoon found Tessa rolling her shoulders to release some tension as she skated through her warm-up, trying not to regret her words to Micah the day before. Oh, not that he'd treated her poorly, but he *had* backed off, asking her a few polite questions about the bleakest time in her life before getting up and taking her hand as they made their way back to Randi's house.

He'd left soon after they'd arrived.

Now, she could feel him watching her as she skated, and he'd been unusually quiet since he'd picked her up this morning.

What did I expect? Did I think he was going to understand why I wanted to off myself? Hell, sometimes I don't even understand it now. But back then, her desperation had been all too real.

After her mother had died, she'd been so alone, feeling so damn worthless that she hadn't wanted to live anymore. She'd shared with Micah how she'd put together a cocktail of medications that she'd been pretty certain would kill her, mainly from a stock she'd had left of her mother's pain and sleeping pills. She'd been ready to go to sleep and never wake up, let the dark pit she'd sunk into take her away.

The only thing that had stopped her at the last minute was Liam. She couldn't leave him all alone, and she knew he'd blame himself for the rest of *his* life if she ended *her own*. She had been selfish, ready to ease her own pain at the expense of her only living close relative.

At the last minute, she'd dumped all of the pills in the toilet and flushed them down the pipes, unwilling to end her pain by causing more for Liam.

Tessa had experienced episodes of depression since her hearing loss, but she'd found herself in her darkest days after her parents were both gone, leaving her alone in a hearing world when she had none. Isolated and feeling separated from the rest of the world, she'd had to battle her way out of the darkness and back into the light. She'd finally escaped after Liam had come home and she'd reached out for counseling. Tessa had never talked about her near-death experience to anyone. How she'd gotten to the point of no return she couldn't fathom now, but she'd been there, ready to take her own life just to escape her anguished existence.

Maybe it had crept up on her a little at a time. Maybe she'd always just gone through the motions after going deaf. The dark cloud had descended when Rick had dumped her, but then she'd had her mom and dad, a reason to stay alive, people who loved her. Too much pain, blow after blow, had rendered her helpless to fight her depression. She was recovered now, for the most part, but she sure as hell knew she couldn't go back there again.

It isn't like I didn't want to give in to Micah, experience the pleasure he could give.

However, she'd grown to like him, and she knew that if she stepped into his fire, she probably wouldn't come out unscathed. There was no future for them. No billionaire with the whole world at his disposal would ever fall for a small-town deaf woman. She wasn't feeling sorry for herself. Tessa was done with that. But she *did* live in reality. Sometimes, for her, the world was much too real.

She didn't need counseling anymore, having worked through the life issues that had spurred her spiral downward. Rationally, she knew she needed to avoid anything that could trigger her sadness if she could. And thinking of Micah Sinclair as anything other than a friend could bring nothing but heartache.

I have to accept the way things are, the way I am now.

As she started skating faster, building up speed, she felt the cool air wafting over her face, her entire body humming with excitement. If nothing else, she could be grateful to Micah for *this*, giving her a means to go back to doing something she loved. Skating was a part of her that had been missing for a long time.

Executing a few double jumps to warm up, she gained speed to finally try a triple. She went into the jump a little off, recognizing immediately where she erred, but it was too late.

She ended up with her ass on the ice.

Brushing off her old skirt as she rose, she could almost hear her former coach's voice in her head, telling her she needed to concentrate.

She gasped as her shoulders were grasped by strong hands, her body suddenly facing Micah.

Her eyes shot to his mouth.

"Christ! I'm sorry. I should have never pushed you into this. Are you hurt?" His face showed nothing but worry for her. He moved his hands up and down her arms.

"I'm fine. If I had a dime for every time I fell on my backside while practicing, I'd be rich," she told him with a laugh. "I was trying a triple. I knew I'd be rusty after almost a decade."

His face was stern as he replied, "Let's go. This is too dangerous. I wish I had never encouraged you to skate again."

Now he thinks I'm fragile, not able to handle anything because I told him I'd experienced a period of my life that I just couldn't handle. Is he worried about my sanity, or my physical well-being?

Tessa grabbed one of his hands. "No. I'm glad you did. I needed this, Micah. And I'm used to falling. It's part of the training."

"I don't want you to get hurt."

It was funny he was saying those words, because her heart ached just from seeing his worried expression. When was the last time any guy cared about whether she was hurt or not? Only her brother, Liam. "It won't kill me," she joked. "I have no doubt I'll fall again and again until I get the routine down."

"I can't watch that. Let's go." He tugged on her hand.

"I'm not done."

"You're done. There's no way you're falling again and again just to perform. What if you break bones?"

She smiled at him. "My coach used to say I bounced well."

He scowled at her. "That's not funny."

She yanked her hand from his. "It's going to happen." Truly, she was floored by his fierce objections. He meant what he said. He wanted her to walk out of the arena and never come back. "I can't quit. You know how many attempts it can take to get something right, and you've done the same thing plenty of times," she said desperately. "Please."

Technically, he could drag her out of the rink. He owned it now.

She needed so much to succeed, not just for the money, but for her psyche.

He hesitated as though he was considering his options. Like Micah Sinclair had any reason to object if she kept falling on her ass? The man did things that would probably make her hair stand on end.

"No. More. Triples." He said the words slowly, as though it was the last thing he wanted to utter, but was doing it anyway.

"Thank you," she replied, knowing she'd have to practice them alone. But she had a key to the rink. She could come here when Micah wasn't around to perfect her more complicated jumps.

"You're thinking about coming here alone, aren't you?"

Busted! She nodded reluctantly, unable to lie to him after all he'd done for her.

"Don't even think about it. You can do simple jumps for your routine. You aren't competing."

Maybe not, but a former Olympic gold medalist should be able to turn in a solid performance. She was still young. "It will be expected," she argued.

"I don't give a shit about what other people expect. I want you healthy."

She gave up for the moment, realizing she was talking to a wall that wasn't going to tumble. She'd place the jumps into her routine, and she'd eventually practice them. If she was being paid for a professional performance, she was going to give the best one she could.

Tessa watched as he skated back to his place by the wall. She started running through her planned routine, smiling just a little every time she passed him.

Micah cared about her safety, and it showed throughout the practice, his attention focused on her every move.

Near the end of practice, Tessa had gained confidence. She risked doing a triple again, knowing in her gut that she could land it. This time she stayed on her feet with just a little bobble instead of with her butt on the ice. Looking quickly over at Micah to see his reaction, Tessa realized that he didn't even know the difference between a double and a triple. He hadn't even noticed.

She released a sigh of relief, knowing she'd been betting on the fact that he wouldn't have a clue exactly what she was doing unless she hit the ground.

Micah felt like he was dangerously close to losing his control, something he very rarely did. In fact, he couldn't remember the last time that he'd totally lost it emotionally. In his line of work, he couldn't afford to *not* keep his focus. But damned if he wasn't near the end of his patience at the moment, and he normally didn't have a limit.

He watched Tessa as she walked into the small living room of Randi's house and took a seat on the other end of the couch he had his ass planted on. After deciding to stay for dinner after practice, he'd used the tiny shower when Tessa had finished, and eaten without either of them communicating during the meal.

This has to end. I have to know more or I'm going to fucking lose it.

He'd bottled up his questions about Tessa's battle with depression, knowing she probably didn't want to talk about it anymore. It was pretty obvious to him that she had come through it. Hell, she was the strongest woman he'd ever met. How many people could survive blow after blow like she had without giving up? Maybe she *almost* had, but the fact was, in the end, she *hadn't*.

He accepted the beer she handed him, noticing that she wasn't imbibing. She was calmly sipping a glass of iced tea.

When he knew she was looking at him he asked, "Are you sure you can handle all this, Tessa?" He didn't want her stressed out. She'd survived enough trauma in her life. Micah wished he had known just how much she'd overcome before he'd talked her into performing again; hell, just the thought of what she'd been through made *him* depressed.

She nodded. "I'm fine, Micah. I'm not going to break. I guess I shouldn't have blurted out everything about myself, but I wanted you to know."

"I wanted to know. It isn't that I didn't want you to tell me. But I'm apprehensive now."

Tessa lifted a brow. "About?"

He wasn't worried she was going to try to kill herself again. In fact, he knew she wouldn't. "You," he answered, because his concern really was just that simple.

She set her iced tea on the table in front of them before she spoke. "You think I'm going to crack again? You think I'm weak and pathetic because I wanted to die rather than face my issues? Do you really think a little stress is going to break me? I competed in front of millions of people when I was a teenager. I learned to keep my emotions under control."

She was indignant and defensive now. It was the last thing Micah had wanted, but he'd screwed up and put her on her guard by not getting to the real issues.

Tessa continued on her tirade. "Okay, yeah, I lost it *once in my life*. I couldn't hear, and I had lost everything: my fiancé, my hearing, my career, and both my parents. I doubt that anybody could even make up that much tragedy if they tried. But it happened, and it happened to me. I was all alone, and for a short time before Liam came home for good, I wondered what I had to live for. I was selfish and only focused on my own drama. I don't like the person I was back then, but I like myself now."

Micah sat his beer on the table and slid across the well-used couch. He breached the distance between them and put his hands on her shoulders. "You never would have killed yourself, Tessa. I know what you think, but if you had really wanted to do it, you would have. And you're not selfish. Even when you hit rock bottom, you still thought about your brother."

Her eyes glistened with tears, one lone droplet falling down her cheek as she blinked. "I wanted to. I felt so alone in the world once my parents were gone. I had friends, but there's a certain isolation you feel when you lose your hearing, a lack of connection that I can't explain."

Micah felt like somebody had punched him in the gut. *Hard.* "What helps?"

She shrugged. "I learned to adjust, to find connections in other ways. But I guess I hadn't learned to compensate back then."

He swiped the tear from her face with his fingers. "You're still afraid? Why?"

Her expression was startled, and she was silent.

There was no question Tessa had healed, but her reaction to him out by the ocean the day before had been extreme. He needed to know why. She was still running away from something, but for the life of him, he wasn't sure what or who she was afraid of.

"It's not you. It's me," she finally whispered huskily. "I became so dependent on Rick when we were together that I'm afraid to ever let myself have any kind of intimate relationship again. It hasn't really been an issue until now because I've never wanted to be with someone as much as I want to be with you, Micah. Not to mention you're the first guy who has actually *wanted* me, even for a casual screw, since I lost my hearing. And I know myself. I can't have uncomplicated sex."

He cupped her face in his hands, his gaze glued to the vulnerable expression on her face as he growled, "Sex with you would *always* be complicated."

He wanted to protect Tessa, shield her from any more disappointments in her life. Yet, he wanted to do so damn much more. If there was one thing he now knew for sure, it was that this woman was *his*, that he needed her to belong to *him*. Maybe subconsciously, he'd always known. But he wasn't fighting it anymore.

His hard-on was pressing against the denim of his jeans, insisting on release, demanding that he claim what belonged to him.

Tessa's fingers trembled as she reached up and put her hands over his that were still framing her face. "It would be terribly complicated. And risky, too."

Micah grinned at her. "I happen to like a certain amount of risk in my life." Maybe that's why Tessa could cause more adrenaline to flow through his body than any sport he'd ever experienced.

"I don't usually take risks," she admitted. "But right now I think maybe I should. I *want* to fly, but I'm afraid of crash-landing."

"Don't be afraid of the fall. *I'll* be there to catch you this time," he told her in a hoarse voice that he barely recognized as his own. Micah desperately needed her to understand he wasn't going anywhere. She said she'd never felt this way before, but then, neither had he. The only thing he knew for sure was that he'd never leave her alone again.

He didn't just want her, he needed her. And he had never needed *anybody*.

She stood up so fast that her body was a blur as his hands fell to the couch, suddenly empty. She strode over to the breakfast bar that separated the small kitchen from the living room, clenching the counter tightly as she said, "I know the deal. Sex only, no strings attached. That's the way you roll, right? But we'll always be friends, and I think I might be able to handle that."

Micah frowned. For him, *all* deals were negotiable with Tessa, and it wasn't just about sex anymore. Hell yeah, he wanted to rip off her clothes and nail her hard and fast, but he wanted her *all in*. Strange . . . since he'd never been willing to do that himself.

He stood and walked over to her, pulling her petite body back against him. He wanted to groan as their bodies collided, the upper curve of her ass rubbing against his painfully erect cock. He turned her around slowly, savoring the feel of her body as she rubbed against him. *Jesus!*

"I don't know the rules anymore," he admitted as she looked up at him. "I just know that I need to bury myself inside of you until neither one of us can think. All of this is new, different. We'd have to make up the rules as we go along."

He pinned her against the counter as he placed his hands on the surface, pissed off at himself that he *couldn't* just walk out the door until he got himself together. That option was completely off the table for him, even though he knew she'd probably be better off if he did.

Tessa didn't need this.

Tessa deserved better.

Tessa needed a guy who didn't live for an adrenaline rush.

She wrapped her arms around his neck. "Then I guess we make our own rules, because I need you right now, Micah. I can't walk away and not experience this, experience you. It would be safer if I did, but I don't think I can. I'd always wonder how it would have been. And I don't want to live with regrets because I was too afraid to find out."

He lost complete control in that moment, her own words sealing her fate. He'd make sure she never wanted to run and never regretted being with him, if it was the last thing on Earth he did.

Maybe he didn't deserve her.

Maybe he was all wrong for her.

Maybe she did deserve someone better.

But the fact was, he couldn't stomach thinking about another man ever touching her again.

For now, she was his, and he intended on claiming her.

The future could fucking take care of itself.

CHAPTER 9

Tessa knew she wasn't thinking with a rational brain at the moment, but she didn't care. As Micah swooped down to capture her mouth, she yielded completely, determined not to think about what would happen later.

She wanted this; she wanted Micah. Every cell in her body was clamoring for him to take her, and she couldn't fight that physical and mental battle anymore. Fear of rejection had been a part of her life for so long that it was hard to let go of it, but what she'd said to him was true. If she didn't reach out and take what she wanted, experience the things she craved, she'd be forever stuck within very limited boundaries.

I don't always need to know what's going to happen. I can live in the moment for once in my life without waiting for something bad to happen.

Screw contentment and safety; she wanted to live.

Her hands found their way to Micah's hair, her breath sighing into his mouth as she raked her short nails over his scalp. When his arms snaked possessively around her body, one big hand landing possessively on her ass and the other around her back, she shivered as their bodies connected. His skin was white-hot, and all she wanted to do was let him scorch her with his fire.

His tongue thrust dominantly in her mouth in between stinging nips to her bottom lip. She moaned, wanting to get closer to him, needing to touch the blazing heat of his skin. His body was like a furnace, and she wanted to jump inside him and be consumed.

"Off," she panted when he released her lips, her hands now tugging at the hem of his T-shirt.

Stepping back, he obliged her, whipping the garment over his head. *Oh. Sweet. Jesus.*

Her heart hammered against the wall of her chest as she stared unabashedly at his defined abs, rippling biceps, and that perfect V that surrounded ripped abdominal muscles that looked like an unmovable wall.

She'd seen him naked, and he'd let her look her fill, but she didn't remember feeling quite this overwhelmed. Maybe because she was past mortification and looking at him with unbridled lust.

Their eyes met as the shirt popped over his forehead, and Tessa's breath caught at the purely carnal, predatory look in his hooded eyes as he dropped it on the floor. His jeans rode low on his hips, a small trail of dark hair stopping disappointingly right at the waistband, the remainder hidden beneath the denim.

Boldly, she stepped forward and flipped the metal button that was keeping her from what she wanted to see, lowering the zipper carefully without breaking eye contact with him.

"I want to see you," she told him insistently.

"Then take what you want," Micah answered, his eyes growing impossibly stormier.

There was something incredibly erotic about a man like Micah offering himself up to her, allowing her the freedom to do anything she wanted with him. She could sense his leashed power, and she felt like she was pulling the tiger's tail right now, but she couldn't stop herself from dropping to her knees and yanking at his jeans and boxer briefs. She wanted to touch him so badly that her hands shook.

Micah helped her, kicking out of the jeans and underwear until he stood in front of her completely nude. Same as before, he seemed to have no problem with being unclothed, and Tessa could see why. He didn't have a damn thing to be shy about. The man was perfection, and the hard-on he was sporting was no small thing, standing hard and thick almost right in front of her face.

Lifting her arms, she put her hands as high as they could reach, letting her palms drift slowly down his muscular stomach, tracing that tantalizing V over and over before finally letting her touch stroke over one rock-hard ass cheek. The muscles between her thighs tightened, and she felt another flood of liquid heat dampen her panties as she fisted his hardness.

She wanted to linger, taste the bead of moisture she saw decorating the head of his cock, but Tessa found herself tugged to her feet reluctantly.

"Not now," Micah told her as he tilted her head up. "I'd never live through it."

She could feel his urgency, see a muscle in his jaw pulsating as he tried to rein in his desperation.

It was the hottest thing she'd ever seen.

"Get naked," he demanded as he reached for the collar of her shirt. Despite his command, he took off her clothes himself, and he wasn't very patient.

Tessa's body quivered as Micah grabbed the top she was wearing and popped the buttons as he tore it down the front, pulling off what was left of the shirt before reaching for the front clasp of her bra.

The desire to feel herself skin-to-skin with him had her shucking her jeans and panties impatiently, then shrugging off the bra he'd left dangling from her arms.

Wrapping her arms around his neck, she buried her face in his neck, taking little tastes of his heated skin as she murmured, "Now."

She felt him shake his head.

"Now," she repeated anxiously, wrapping her legs around his waist, urging his hard erection closer to her needy core.

Supporting her ass, he walked to the counter and sat her down on the low surface. They were almost face-to-face.

Her hands never stopped moving, the feel of his body beneath her fingers so sensual that she couldn't stop touching him. "Please."

Desire was racing through her body, the need to have him inside her. Micah resisted even though he looked like he was ready to go caveman on her and fuck her until she screamed for mercy.

She startled when his hands cupped her breasts, his thumbs circling around the hardened nipples, playing over them until she started to whimper.

Rick had never really touched her breasts; Micah seemed to worship them.

Grasping her wrists, he put her hands on the surface behind her, her ass sitting on the edge of the counter with all of the space behind her. Tightening her legs around him, she was frustrated that the surface was too high to make contact with his cock.

Before she could register her frustration, his mouth was on her nipples, sucking one of them into his mouth, biting lightly and then soothing it with his tongue.

Heat shot through her belly, her body registering a sensation she'd never felt before. "Oh, God. Micah." She squirmed, but he was persistent, alternating from nipple to nipple until they were diamond-hard, sensitive peaks. He bit just hard enough to make the pain pleasurable, especially when he soothed it with his wicked tongue.

Finally, just when Tessa thought she was going to lose her mind with frustrated lust, Micah pushed her back on the counter, untangled her legs from his waist, and spread her thighs. It left her feet dangling from the counter, and she opened her eyes, having forgotten at what point of pleasure she'd actually closed them.

She looked for Micah just in time to get a top view of his golden head lowering between her open thighs. Slamming her eyes closed again, her breath hitched . . . waiting. She screamed as his scorching tongue parted her folds, delving, searching relentlessly for the tiny bundle of nerves he was seeking. He found it and ruthlessly teased the hardened bud, causing Tessa to arch her back in tormented pleasure.

The sensation was intimate and decadent, and she felt herself beginning to float on a high she'd never experienced before, her body being taken over by Micah's merciless mouth.

She speared her fingers into his hair. Begging. Pleading. Needing release with a ferocity she'd never known existed.

"Please, Micah. I can't take any more," she whimpered almost incoherently, but she knew he heard every sound that escaped her lips.

She was jolted from her haze of pleasure as he pulled her up just in time to see his tormented expression, then watched as he retrieved a condom from the pocket of his jeans with lightning speed and quickly rolled it on.

"Now!" She caught the word as her eyes flew to his lips. "Wrap your legs around me."

She instantly moved her lower limbs and tangled them around his hips as he grasped the flesh of her ass tightly with his strong fingers. Taking a few steps, he pinned her body against the wall.

Tightening her arms around his neck, all she could feel was the raw, sensual, pleasurable sensation of her nipples colliding with the heat of his hard chest, the peaks so swollen that she moaned as the rest of their flesh met and melded together so tightly that she didn't know where he ended and she began.

"Yes," she moaned as Micah drove up into her tight, wet sheath in one hard thrust, his hands guiding her down with his grasp on her hips and ass.

He fucked her hard and fast, like a man who had been starved of carnal pleasure for a very long time. Tessa ground with his pumping motions, the strained muscles in her channel gripping him tightly every time he impaled her.

Her hands fisted in his hair, and she pulled his mouth tighter against hers as he kissed her, his tongue mimicking every thrust of his cock.

Micah's powerful body surged harder and deeper, and Tessa knew she was about to climax hard. There had been so much teasing, and she'd been so close to orgasm when Micah had gone down on her, that she couldn't burn much hotter without exploding into a mass of incendiary flames.

His chest was vibrating in what Tessa instinctively knew was a low groan of pleasure.

Climax rocked her body as Micah kept slamming into her over and over, sending her tumbling over the edge of the imaginary cliff she'd been standing on in a very precarious position. She soared as her orgasm shot through her entire being.

"Oh, God. Micah. Yes." She clasped his shoulders tightly, her nails digging into his upper back. Her head dropped, her face resting against his damp neck as her muscles tightened and released over his pummeling cock.

His big body shuddered as he found his own release, and Tessa hugged him fiercely against her as he thrust one last time and the tremors stopped.

Her body was still humming with pleasure as he carried her out of the living room and into her bedroom. When he disconnected their bodies and laid her gently on the bed, she wanted to protest, but remembered he had to dispose of his condom, and they couldn't stay joined forever.

He was back from the bathroom before she even caught her breath, and he lowered his massive body onto the mattress beside her, then circled his strong arm around her waist. He pulled until she was almost sprawled on top of him.

Her eyes shot to his mouth in time to catch his one-word comment. "Complicated."

Then he grinned at her happily, not looking the least bit troubled by the fact that their coupling had been mind-blowing—at least for her.

Her heart lifted, and she smiled back at him, reaching up to smooth an unruly lock of his hair that always seemed to be on his forehead. Then, she nodded. "Complicated," she agreed.

He fingered a lock of her crazy curls. "If that's what complicated is like, I'd have no problem if it gets *really* complex."

Tessa let out a surprised laugh. "You think you can top what just happened?" Sex with Micah was almost surreal, so she didn't know how he could outdo what had just occurred.

He gave her a fake scowl. "That was the work of a desperate man. Sloppy. I wanted to make you come first with my mouth. I wanted to keep devouring you, Tessa. I wanted to wring every drop of pleasure I could from your body before I got inside you. I knew I wouldn't last long."

She covered his lips with her fingers. "Don't. It was amazing. I wouldn't have wanted it any other way."

He was grinning again. "Hard, fast, and up against the wall?"

"Yes."

"Most women would complain."

She winked at him. "I'm not complaining, stud. Most men couldn't lift a woman up against a wall." Tessa was serious. How many guys could really do a woman that way? It had been honest and raw. Maybe that was what made it so special.

"I couldn't wait. That's how bad I wanted you, Tessa. I have since the moment I saw you. I felt like a horny teenager. I wanted to bend you over the sink in the bathroom and take you right there in the guesthouse."

She looked at him in surprise. "You did not," she protested.

"I did. I wanted to go caveman on your beautiful ass." His hand moved down and squeezed her rear. "I'm not used to having that kind of reaction to a woman."

"You had a serious relationship once." Tessa knew he'd been in one committed relationship years ago.

He nodded. "Once," he agreed.

"Tell me," she asked, knowing he was being deliberately vague.

"I met Anna in college, and we lived together after we finished school. She was from a wealthy family, so I pretty much knew she didn't hook up with me because of my money. She hated my interest in sky-diving and extreme sports. She kept waiting for me to settle down, but I never did. I traveled a lot, and she didn't really want a career. I think she was ready to get married and have kids. College was just a necessary step before getting married."

"You didn't want to marry her?" Tessa asked curiously, realizing that trying to contain Micah would be like trying to pull a star down from the sky and stuff it into a bottle.

"I cared about her, and I thought we'd get married eventually, but I was still building my skills and my own company. We were young, and I guess I didn't stop to consider how she felt. After a few years, she got tired of waiting and settled down with one of my friends who was content to be wealthy and eventually take control of his father's business."

"She cheated on you?" Tessa could tell from his subdued expression that it hadn't been an amicable breakup.

"I came home unexpectedly from a business trip and found them together. In our bed," he told her flatly. "I was pretty clueless. It hit me pretty hard. It took me a while to realize that I had nothing to offer *any* woman."

"That's not true," Tessa replied indignantly. "She was a snake. You don't screw another man in your current boyfriend's bed. I don't care if she was going to eventually break up with you or not. It's disgusting."

"So you think I deserved to be let down easily?" Micah teased.

"I think she was crazy for not traveling with you. If she didn't want her own career, she could have helped you build your company. You were both young. She could have seen the world before she decided to get married." Tessa sighed, knowing if she'd had Micah's devotion, she certainly wouldn't have thrown it away. Besides, she couldn't think of anything more satisfying than traveling around with a man she was crazy about. Micah would be fun, and although she'd traveled some places when she was young and competing, she'd never been able to see anything. She'd been there for one reason and one reason only: to compete.

She'd gone a few places with Rick, but he wasn't a pleasant travel companion, and he certainly hadn't wanted to play tourist.

"Is that what you'd do, Tessa? Support a guy you cared about?"

She looked at his questioning expression. "Of course. If he supported me, then I'd support him. I can't claim to be an expert, but relationships are give-and-take, I think." She paused before she ran a comforting hand down Micah's cheek. "I'm sorry she hurt you."

"I'm over it," he replied.

She tilted her head and surveyed his expression. "I don't think you are. I don't think you trust women much anymore."

"Maybe I've just never found the right one to trust," he answered, putting a hand over hers as it came to rest on his chest. "Having a woman who can live with my career choice isn't easy, either."

Tessa shrugged. "You are who you are, Micah. I'm not saying it would be easy for a woman who cared about you not to worry, but she'd have to accept that *you* wouldn't be *you* if you weren't doing what you loved."

"I don't do many BASE jumps anymore, and I've had to cut some things because my priorities are different. I want to make extreme sports safer. But I could never give up my skydiving team, and I like to push some limits."

"Slowing down?" she answered teasingly. "Getting old?"

He frowned at her. "No. I've just seen too many friends and acquaintances die by doing dumb jumps and not having safe-enough equipment. Finding a safe place to BASE jump is getting harder. It's illegal in most of the best places to jump."

"So you leap from a perfectly good airplane instead?"

"Don't knock it until you try it. My team is pretty damn good, one of the best in the world. And there's no feeling like a free fall."

"Actually, I always wanted to try it. When I was younger, I didn't have time. Then when I lost my hearing, I knew it was never going to happen." Skydiving had been one of the things she'd always wanted to experience but never had. She guessed maybe it was one of those things that looked fun while she was watching it, but fear might have kept her from executing a jump. There was something a little bit crazy about jumping out of an airplane and relying on a parachute to keep from becoming a human pancake.

"So, do it. All skydivers are deaf once they leave the plane anyway. It's not like you need to hear. You can't hear anything except the roar of the wind."

Tessa shook her head. "Lessons are expensive, and I would have been stepping outside my comfort zone. I'm not sure I could do it."

"You could go with me," he suggested. "I'm an instructor and I've done thousands of jumps. We could go tandem. I'd never risk your safety. If I wasn't confident with taking you up, I wouldn't."

Oh, he was cocky when it came to his skills, but that confidence amused Tessa. She knew it came from experience, and she had no doubt Micah knew what he was doing. "I'd have to trust you first," she contemplated jokingly. "But I'd love to fly with you someday."

He moved so fast that Tessa squealed. In seconds, she was on her back with him on top of her, loosely restraining her wrist at the side of her head. "You'll trust me," he told her, a small, confident smile on his face.

"I suppose. You've already taken me flying once," she joked.

"Get ready, woman. We're about to do another practice run."

She actually giggled as he began to lower his head to capture her mouth. All thought of skydiving left her mind as Micah kissed her, taking her to heights she'd never even imagined without ever leaving the bed.

CHAPTER 10

Micah was feeling unusually relaxed when he went into town the next day. He'd been willing to blow off their morning run, but Tessa had nagged him into getting his ass into gear. Hell, he was either getting old, or he was worn out from exercising in the most pleasant of ways all night long with Tessa. He was pretty sure it was the second option, since it had been a while since he'd had sex. With a smirk, he realized he'd made up for lost time last night.

After their run, they'd showered and had lunch, then he'd gone to the rink with Tessa. Dropping her off, he told her he needed to run back to the guesthouse on the Peninsula to get some clothing. But he made a stop first, one he wasn't looking forward to making.

He stopped in front of Sullivan's Steak and Seafood when he saw that the place was closed. Glancing at his watch, he realized they'd be open for dinner business very shortly. Micah's eyes scanned the chipped paint on the outside of the building, wondering when it had last been painted. Between the salt water and the humidity, the exterior had taken a beating.

Putting his hand on the door handle, he turned it and then pushed hard on the door, surprised to see that it opened.

Doesn't anybody lock their doors here?

He'd had to remind Tessa to lock up every time he left Randi's old house. She did it, but she rolled her eyes at him every single time, reminding him that he wasn't in New York. Hell, maybe he was paranoid, but he'd never been in a town where half the people never locked their doors.

He entered the restaurant and closed the door quietly behind him.

As he headed for the kitchen, where he was hearing some chopping sounds, he looked around the small restaurant, noting the ragged chairs and slightly tilting tables. The walls were lacking some chips of paint just like the outside of the building. Strangely, with all of the nautical décor, it looked almost normal for the place to appear somewhat old and tired.

"We're closed." Liam's voice sounded from the order window.

"I know," Micah answered as he strolled over to the kitchen door and entered without an invitation. Now, face-to-face with Tessa's brother, he added, "I wanted to talk to you."

"I *said* . . . we're closed. Get the hell out of here," Liam answered stubbornly.

Micah shook his head, resting his hip against the counter as he crossed his arms, staying several feet away from Liam. "I can't. I have a business proposition to make."

"I don't need anything from you, Sinclair," Liam growled as he went back to what he'd been doing before Micah had entered: removing lobster meat from the shell and slicing it. He tossed the cut pieces into a plastic container, probably in preparation for all of the lobster rolls he'd sell later.

"I think you might," Micah drawled, watching Liam as he worked.

He had to admit, Liam knew his lobster. Tessa's brother was making short work of his task in a hurry.

"Doubtful," Liam answered, chopping a little bit harder at the seafood than he needed to.

"I want to form a partnership, invest money into refurbishing your building, equipment, and whatever else you need."

Liam stopped working and glared at him. "What the hell for? I don't need you. Why are you here, anyway?" He cocked an accusing brow. "Stay away from Tessa."

Micah grinned. Liam was a little late for *that* warning. "We've already been together. A lot."

He stopped smiling as Liam lunged for him, grabbing the collar of his polo shirt. "Did you touch her?"

Jesus! This guy is uptight. And I thought I was bad.

"It's none of your damn business what we did. Tessa is an adult," Micah growled as he dislodged Liam's hand from his apparel. "Keep control of your damn temper, and keep your hands off me. I'm here to talk."

Tessa's brother turned red with rage. "She isn't a woman that you can use and then toss away. She's been there, and doesn't need to do it again. She might be old enough to know better, but she has an impulsive streak sometimes."

"I know," Micah answered as he straightened the collar of his shirt. "And I have no intentions of tossing her anywhere. I care about her." *Too damn much!*

Liam let out a disgusted male snort. "Whatever. Just take your ass back to where you belong."

Micah ignored his comment. "I want to put the money into the restaurant, get it fixed up."

"Why?" Liam was eyeing him suspiciously.

"The locals love this place, and it's worth renovating."

"I can do it myself."

"Then why is Tessa busting her ass to find the funds to fix this place? She counts every damn penny she earns."

"Our parents left us their house, which is paid for, and a decent sum of money," Liam snarled at Micah. "The last thing I need is *your money.* I've told Tessa before that we have funds. She just refuses to even look at our joint account. Says she wants me to have it."

"So she doesn't need to work her cleaning jobs?"

"Hell, no. If she wasn't so stubborn, she'd see that we have the money. But she won't look. Mom and Dad left us a nice inheritance. We do very well with the restaurant, and I do some consulting on the side. I live rent-free and I put money away. Most of my problem is time. It's hard to close the restaurant for renovations, but I'll do it in the winter."

"What kind of consulting?" Micah asked curiously.

"I worked in TV and films doing special effects and some stunt work," Liam answered in a graveled voice. "If they need advice, I consult. I used to patent products I made for my line of work. I make a lot in royalties. The last thing I need is more money."

Interesting. If Liam and I didn't hate each other's guts, we could probably be friends.

Obviously, Liam Sullivan's expertise was engineering, and doing calculated stunts and work on special effects. If Micah wasn't here for a far different reason, he'd be bombarding the guy with questions.

"I want to help Tessa," Micah answered stubbornly. Even if she didn't need his money, he wanted to take the stress of refurbishing the restaurant off her.

"The last thing my sister needs is your kind of help, Sinclair," Liam snarled, his face still flushed with anger.

"Much as I hate to disagree with you, you're wrong." Micah's tone was dripping with sarcasm. "She's skating again, something she should have done a long time ago."

Liam snorted. "She can't skate."

"Something you feel is your fault," Micah said lightly.

"It *is* my fault," Liam grumbled. "And how the hell is she skating? The rink is closed."

"I opened it. She's regaining her skills, and she's going to skate a routine for a reunion performance of Olympic champions in just a few weeks."

Liam stepped forward and grabbed Micah's shirt again. "What in the hell are you doing to her? She can't skate. I'm proud of the way she's learned to function in a hearing world, but she's still working with a hell of a handicap. What happens when she fails, dumbass? Huh? Are you going to be around to take care of her when her world falls apart again?"

Pissed off now, Micah used his forearm to force Liam to release his grip, then promptly punched the big man in the face. It propelled Liam's body back against the counter of the preparation area.

Micah shook his hand, irritated that he'd bruised his knuckles on Tessa's jackass of a brother. "I asked you nicely once. I don't *ask* a second time," he warned Liam with a growl. "You might be a little bigger, but I've practiced martial arts since I was a kid, and I learned my fighting skills from some of the best in extreme sports. That was a warning. Touch me again and I'll actually kick your ass."

"Bastard," Liam rasped, but he strode across the kitchen to get a clean towel for his bleeding nose, holding pressure on his face as he walked back to stand in front of Micah with a murderous glare. "You're fast," he confessed with a grimace as he held the towel to his face.

Micah shrugged. "I can be even faster. I didn't come here to fight with you. I came here to help. Whether you can get it through your thick head or not, your sister certainly can skate. Losing her hearing didn't affect her abilities on the ice. Yes, she's rusty from lack of practice, but she's improving, and she'll be damn good by the time she appears in New York. This is something she wanted, something she needed. Nobody was forcing her to try."

Micah inwardly flinched just a little because he *had* challenged her, but Tessa had been more than capable of calling him on his dare.

"How did you get the rink back open?" Liam asked gruffly.

"I own much of the property on that side of town. I also own the rink and Randi's old home. I encouraged Tessa to skate again. It was a big part of her life that was missing."

Liam shot Micah a threatening look as he answered, "You'll end up breaking her, Sinclair. And when you do, I'll fucking kill you."

"It's not possible for me to break her. Without skating, Tessa was never whole."

"She was happy," Liam insisted.

"Happy? With you breathing down her neck, telling her what she could and couldn't do? Dealing with your sense of guilt? You think she was happy?" Micah's voice rose automatically until he was almost yelling at Liam to try to get through to him.

"I'm the only one left to protect her," Liam bellowed.

"Not anymore," Micah told him in a lower, more dangerous tone.

"You think she carries my guilt?" Liam asked in a confused voice.

"Of course. She feels guilty that you feel guilty." It sounded strange, but there it was . . . the truth. Liam could take it or leave it. "You need to get over something that wasn't your fault. Nobody could have known Tessa would get sick, or that she'd go deaf. I get it. If you'd known, you would have been there. But you couldn't be there and it happened."

"I was supposed to be there—"

"But you had responsibilities, a job to finish. You made the same decision any person would make who cared about their job. You cancelled. I would have done the same damn thing."

Liam slammed his fist down on a nearby counter. "Fuck! I don't understand why it had to happen at all. Not to somebody like Tessa. She's never hurt anybody in her entire life. She didn't deserve it." He strode to the back of the kitchen and threw away the towel he'd been using, his face a dark mask of remorse as he returned.

For that brief moment, Micah could sympathize with the man in front of him. Tessa *hadn't* deserved *any* of the multiple shitty things that had happened to her, but it was reality. "She's alive, and she's handled her situation with more courage than most people would."

"That's why I need to be there for her. Don't you get it? I want her to stay safe. With Mom and Dad gone, she's my only family."

Micah nodded abruptly. "Yeah, I get it. But you're not keeping her safe. You're suffocating her now. Tessa is capable of nearly everything a hearing woman can do. She's smart, and she's talented. If you keep holding her back, you're shortchanging her."

"Can she really skate?" Liam asked, sounding uncomfortable.

"Like a champion," Micah answered.

Liam shook his head in confusion. "I thought she needed me."

"She did. She still does, as a supportive sibling. She just doesn't need you to tell her what to do anymore. But she doesn't want to hurt you, so she's never going to tell you that." Micah hesitated before adding, "I'd still like to help with the restaurant. It means a lot to Tessa, and it means something to the community."

Liam shook his head again. "Dude, when I said I didn't need your help, I meant it. I haven't fixed up the place because it's always so busy, but it's not from lack of funds. I make damn good money consulting and from royalties, and the restaurant pulls in a really good profit. Tessa and I don't spend much money because we're always working. I didn't want my sister picking up extra jobs, but she said she was bored. I thought it was what she wanted. Even after we renovate, we'll both have a sizable amount of money in the joint business account, and we have equal interest in a house here that's paid for. She'll be far from broke. I'll break our funds apart and deposit her money into her account. I guess it's the only way she's ever going to understand that she's well set up, and so am I. And I'll get the renovation work scheduled now that it's past tourist season. I'll talk to my sister and make her understand that she has a sizable savings this time."

Micah nodded and crossed his arms in front of him again. "Good. Because the first two times we met, one of us was naked because of her side jobs. I don't want her meeting another unclothed guy again unless it's me."

Liam reached for him. "Are you fucking her?" he growled.

Micah batted Liam's hand away. "Don't do it, man." He met Liam's angry stare with an equally irritated expression of his own. "It's none of your business what's happening between me and your sister, but for the record, I don't plan on leaving her. *Ever.*" He stressed the last word through gritted teeth. "I care about her like I've never cared about any other woman."

Liam circled Micah for a moment before grinding out, "I don't trust you."

Micah smirked at Tessa's brother. "Maybe not now. But you will. Tessa wants to see you doing what you love. Do you want to go back to what you were doing before, full time?"

"Hell, no. I loved my job, but this restaurant is our legacy. Amesport is home for me, now. There's nowhere else I'd rather be. I wouldn't ever go back to the city. Too damn crowded."

Micah nodded. "Good. Maybe you should tell your sister that. She thinks you sacrificed everything for her."

"I didn't sacrifice anything," Liam grumbled. "I want to be here."

"Liam!" A female voice called from the entrance of the restaurant right before a bubbly brunette came waltzing into the kitchen. The woman stopped for a moment, her expression turning from a carefree smile to a frown. "What happened to you? You're bleeding."

Liam held up a hand. "I'm fine. Can you finish doing the lobster meat for the rolls?"

"Um . . . sure," she answered cautiously, moving slowly over to the prep area.

Micah watched as Liam's eyes followed the female, a woman who obviously worked in the restaurant, the big guy's eyes softening as he stared in the direction of the prep area.

"She's attractive," Micah said quietly enough that the brunette couldn't hear him.

"She's young," Liam answered, tearing his gaze away from the woman and back to Micah.

"Over twenty-one, I'd say," Micah observed.

"Not by much," Liam replied unhappily.

Micah pulled out several tickets that he'd asked his assistant to send him, and handed two to Liam. He put the rest back into his pocket as he said, "Maybe she'd like to come to New York to watch Tessa skate. Here are two tickets for the charity performance. I hope you're coming."

Tessa's brother snatched them from Micah's hand. "Of course I'm coming. I just hope you're right or I *will* kill you," he grumbled.

"Tessa's excited about performing again. Try to be happy for her instead of being a damn buzzkill, will you?" The last thing Micah wanted was for Tessa to be wondering how her brother was feeling on her big night.

He turned to leave the restaurant, but Liam again reached out a large hand to detain him, this time lightly grasping his forearm.

"You sure she can do this?" There was concern in Liam's voice now. "What if she falls on her ass?"

"Then she'll get back up and keep skating," Micah replied, shaking Liam's hand from his arm. "Just like she always has," he added, walking toward the front door.

Micah wasn't about to let Liam know he had the same fears. He didn't want Tessa to fall, either, because he didn't want her hurt. But he damn well had the confidence that she could handle herself on the ice, even if she stumbled.

He'd had to rein himself in many times, but he realized that he couldn't hold her back any more than he'd like being kept from what he loved.

If she thinks I didn't know the difference between a double jump and a triple jump, she's wrong.

Micah knew she'd pulled off that triple in the rink, but that was the moment that he realized he couldn't stop her from doing what she loved because of his irrational fear of her getting injured. Yeah, he'd had to grind his teeth, but he was trying to set her free, not keep her confined in her small comfort zone.

He didn't look back, allowing Liam to stew for a while. The guy needed time to think about what Tessa really needed, and it wasn't an overprotective brother.

Me. She fucking needs me.

Maybe Tessa deserved better than a man who lived for an adrenaline rush, but Micah would be damned if he was going to let another guy touch her ever again.

He prepared to exit with a heavy tug on the door, feeling it stick for a moment before it finally gave way and opened.

"Mr. Sinclair? Oh, my, you're finally here."

Micah pulled the door closed behind him and faced the two little old ladies standing right in front of him.

With their short gray hair and similar heights, Micah could hardly tell the two women apart. He looked at both of their smiling faces, knowing Beatrice Gardener was on the left only because of her more flamboyant, colorful dress. Elsie Renfrew was next to her in a more conservative dress and sensible flat shoes, staring at him as if she was surprised to see him. Beatrice, dressed in a flowing, bright-purple skirt and a lighter-colored top, didn't seem the least bit shocked at his presence in Amesport.

He nodded. "Ladies," he acknowledged politely. He barely knew either woman, except for the fact that Beatrice had gifted him with a rock that he oddly carried in his pocket even now. He looked at her and asked about her greeting. "How did you even know I was going to be here?" Hell, he hadn't even known he was leaving New York for some downtime until recently.

"Because your destiny is here," Beatrice told him matter-of-factly. "Of course I knew you'd come. You can fight your fate, but you have to eventually give in. The stone should help. Have you seen Tessa yet?"

Micah looked at the older woman in surprise. "You think Tessa is my destiny?"

It was Elsie who nodded. "She's known for a long time. She's very in tune with you Sinclairs."

He'd written both of the women off as eccentrics. He'd met them at Hope's winter party, and then again at Evan's wedding. They were harmless enough, but neither one of them ever made much sense.

Elsie was respected, a governing member of the community. Strangely, Beatrice seemed to command people's attention, too, but he'd never figured out why. She was a business owner, some New Age store called Natural Elements or some such thing, if he recalled correctly, but Micah didn't put any stock into her acclaimed foresight and ESP. He'd always thought the people of Amesport just humored her because she was elderly.

He dug into his front jeans pocket and pulled out the black stone Beatrice had gifted him. "Because of this?" he questioned Beatrice, opening his palm, noting that the stone seemed strangely . . . warm.

Now I'm imagining some strange shit. Of course the rock is warm. It was in my pocket!

Beatrice shook her head. "Not *because of* the Apache tear. Tessa has always been your soul mate, your destiny. I gave you both the stone so you could recognize it."

Micah was silent for a moment before he finally spoke. "What are you doing here?"

"Well, we're going to eat, of course," Beatrice told him as though he should have known what they were doing. "The best lobster in the area."

Micah felt the hair at the back of his neck rise, and he slapped a hand to his nape, disconcerted by both sets of knowing eyes on him at the moment. "Uh . . . sure. Don't let me stop you, ladies." He leaned over and flipped the sign beside the door to "Open," and then motioned them forward. It was time. Liam should have opened for business by now.

He shoved the stone back in his pocket, still wondering at the fact that Beatrice had apparently paired him with Tessa before he'd even figured everything out for himself. To be honest, it was a little bit creepy to him now, but there was a part of him that was fascinated. The self-proclaimed matchmaker had done the same thing with all of his Sinclair cousins. Was it possible that she really knew . . . ?

Micah put a gentle hand on Beatrice's shoulder as she went to pass. "What about Julian and Xander?"

I can't believe I just asked that!!

Beatrice beamed up at him. "Julian's fate is already decided. Xander is a little more unclear. I've never met him, but he's very troubled. But I have faith that he'll eventually come around."

"Are you sure?" Although he didn't totally believe in the woman's power to see the future, any reassurance about Xander was welcome, even if it wasn't accurate. "Who do you predict for Julian?"

Beatrice's expression turned thoughtful as she reached up and patted Micah's cheek. "Take care of yourself and Tessa. Your brothers will work everything out for themselves in time."

Micah gaped after the two women as they waved and disappeared into the dilapidated restaurant.

Shaking his head in denial, he finally started walking, still feeling the warmth of the stone in his pocket as he told himself that there was no such thing as fate and destiny . . . and soul mates.

By the time he had reached his truck, he'd almost convinced himself that the two women were just eccentric.

If only the stone in his pocket would stop burning, he'd feel a hell of a lot more assured.

CHAPTER 11

The next few days were all about pushing her limits for Tessa. She'd seen Liam, but her brother hadn't said much about her decision to skate again. In fact, he'd consciously encouraged her, which had frankly surprised the hell out of her.

Micah had given up on the guesthouse and had brought an overnight bag with him just the day before. She was guessing neither one of them wanted to miss an opportunity to explore the heat that sizzled between them. Tessa knew she didn't. Now that she'd committed herself to living in the moment and enjoying every single minute she could get with Micah, she was going to take full advantage.

That was, until today.

They had begun the morning as they usually did with a morning run, and then she'd gone to the rink. She was progressing well, her routine together, including her complex jumps and sequences. They had the music, a recording of a choreographed performance she already knew. When she passed by Micah at the sidelines, he gave her signals on how to correct herself if she was off the beat of the music, running behind or ahead of the audio. Mentally, she had to adjust the music in her head, but so far it had worked out well.

Micah had promised to be by her side in New York, and Tessa was getting less and less nervous. She wasn't competing anymore, so now she could skate just for enjoyment, for the joy of being back on the ice.

Now Micah gave her a thumbs-up, his hands in front of her, signaling that he was ready.

"I can't believe I'm really doing this," she whispered to herself, looking down at the approximately fourteen-thousand-foot drop right outside that open door of a perfectly sound airplane. What was she thinking? Did she really want to jump out of a plane that was perfectly safe and solid beneath her feet?

They left the skating rink earlier now, basically only needing to go through the routine and make sure it all went off well. Then, Micah would take her somewhere to do something crazy. It had gone on like that for two days. This was day number three.

She'd loved parasailing with him. There was a small company in town that had offered it for a while now, but she'd never actually done it. But then, she was comfortable at safe heights, and had grown up on the water.

Then there had been the rock climbing yesterday, and learning from one of the best free solo climbers in the world—a title that belonged to Micah—was extraordinary. Not that he'd let her go without safety equipment, and she highly doubted that experience had been much of a rush for him. The climb had been pretty tame. After all, they hadn't gone far. Nevertheless, Tessa had been pretty damn proud when she'd gotten to the top of the small rock formation.

However, she *was* terrified today. Yeah, she was enjoying doing things outside her comfort zone, but *this* was a little much.

She could feel the reassurance of Micah's big body behind her, her smaller form attached to him by a harness, straps at her chest, shoulders, and legs.

He'll do all the work. I just have to not fight him and remember his instructions. I need to relax.

"I'm not sure if I'm ready," she finally answered loudly, knowing the plane was noisy. Micah had already told her that she needed to yell to be heard over the noise of the aircraft. Cautiously, she peeked out the door once again. "What if I forget something?"

He handed her a note, one that he'd obviously written before they had left the ground.

Trust me. We'll be connected, and I won't let you fall.

The hastily written words on a small scrap of paper nearly brought tears to her eyes. How had he known she'd be scared once she was strapped to him, unable to see his face?

She was tandem skydiving with Micah. He'd ordered the plane and they had a safe drop zone. Still, she felt like a million or more butterflies were trying to escape her stomach.

After some intense and quick instruction, they'd been on their way up in a plane piloted by someone Micah knew well. He was a master skydiver and had the special credentials for tandem jumps. He'd also made sure to mention that they were using Xtreme Dive equipment, the best skydiving gear available, in his opinion, which had made Tessa laugh at his arrogance.

It didn't surprise her that he'd done thousands of jumps safely: solo, tandem, and group jumping and formation. Micah was the leader of one of the most elite jumping teams in the world.

This jump was probably nothing more than routine for him. But Tessa was more nervous than she'd been skating in the Olympics. Most figure skaters didn't look death in the face performing their sport.

It's safe. He told me about the safety record of skydiving. It's rare to have a death among regular jumpers.

It all came down to the few words he'd written; it came down to trust. Did she trust him?

She tucked the note into a small zippered pocket of the protective jumpsuit she was wearing.

Then, she gave him a confident thumbs-up. The truth was, she *did* trust him, and the thoughtful note he'd scribbled before they'd gotten into the air just reinforced her bond with him. She'd take this leap with him, just like she'd taken several leaps in the past weeks with him. There was no one she'd rather be with, even if she was jumping out of a very nice plane.

Micah didn't waste any time letting her know they were going as he once again gave her the "go" sign himself, and they both tumbled out the door of the plane.

Her heart lodged in her throat as they exited, her body attached to the front of him, both of them falling at what seemed like an alarming rate. She automatically put her arms out in the correct position once they cleared the plane, a silent scream in her head as she felt the air rushing by them. Their bodies continued to drop at a rate of speed she never could have imagined.

The free fall only lasted for a minute or so, but she finally embraced the rapid plummet toward Earth a few seconds after they'd started to descend. If she was going to die, there was nothing she could do about it, and she wanted to enjoy her last moments.

Right now, Micah was as deaf as she was, or so she'd been told. Not only were they wearing protective helmets, but when one was falling to the ground at over a hundred miles an hour, it was hard to hear anything but the wind rushing past the body. Micah had told her that a skydiver was unable to hear anything but the air during free fall.

Her heart was racing as she looked through a pair of protective goggles, feeling like she was flying, floating through the air like a bird. Seconds ticked by as the ground got closer and closer, Tessa soaking up the exhilaration of their tandem free fall. Never in her life had she felt so uninhibited, her body racing with adrenaline as their parachute deployed and Micah began to guide them to the best place to land.

Her wonder of the ride didn't end as they started to glide, drifting at a height that she should find terrifying, but didn't. She was still nestled against Micah as they grew closer and closer to the ground, and she felt . . . safe.

Moving her legs aside as they got ready to land, he ended up on his feet, coming to a gentle stop.

Working around the parachute, he was able to free them both in a very short amount of time. Tessa pulled her helmet off as she turned to face him, immediately noticing his enormous grin.

The entire jump had only lasted approximately five minutes, but the experience was right up there with some of the most amazing moments in her entire life.

"Oh, my God. That was fantastic," she yelled at him, unable to hold back her emotions.

"Were you scared?" he asked by signing, then pulled off his own helmet and unzipped his jumpsuit to his waist.

"Terrified," she answered. "But I was okay once we were out of the plane."

"It's normal to be scared the first time," he replied.

"Can I learn to jump by myself?" she questioned excitedly.

"We'll see," he said, his smile starting to be replaced by a contemplative look. "I was pretty happy with that position myself."

She smiled at his suggestive comment, watching as their pickup drove toward them, men exiting the truck and starting to collect the parachute that Micah had already slid off his back.

Tessa wanted to thank him, but how did she thank a man for literally giving her back her life? Micah had never treated her differently because she had lost her hearing. He pushed her buttons, pushed her limits, but he never saw her deafness as a handicap. It was the first time anybody had ever treated her quite the same way they had when she could hear.

As soon as he was free of his protective gear, she threw herself into his arms and hugged him. He wrapped his arms around her as though he understood every emotion she couldn't voice as he held her closely, so tightly that she never wanted him to let go.

***

A few hours later, Tessa sighed as she let warm water flow over her body, happy that she finally didn't stink. After a morning run, a workout at the arena, and then their skydiving escapade, she knew she smelled ripe. She'd hit the shower as soon as she and Micah had walked through the door of Randi's old home. Lingering because the water felt so good, she squeaked as Micah opened the door of the enclosure and stepped in like he owned the place, which he actually did.

It was a small shower stall, but Tessa didn't care. She stepped aside and let Micah wash, content to watch him and his perfectly sculpted body as he cleaned up. When he was done, he wrapped an arm around her and pulled her against him, and she snaked her arms around his neck.

"I never get tired of seeing you naked," she admitted, looking up at his handsome face as a droplet of water dripped from his wet hair.

He didn't say a word as his mouth lowered to hers in a scorching kiss that made every tangible thought in her head vanish.

All she could do was feel the heat of Micah's mouth and the need that fired in her soul as she connected with his raw desire.

"I can never touch you enough," he answered as soon as he broke off his passionate embrace, his palms cupping her wet breasts.

"Then touch me," she pleaded.

She tilted her head as his lips explored the slick skin of her neck, giving him as much access to her as he wanted to take.

Tessa knew she was getting addicted to Micah, but it was an intoxicating feeling that she refused to give up. She let her palms slide down his muscular torso, not stopping her descent until she could finally grasp his engorged cock. "I want this," she insisted, dropping slowly to her knees in the cramped shower.

He usually protested whenever she wanted to taste him, nudging her away so he could bury himself inside her. This time, her heart accelerated as his hands speared through her hair, letting her do what she'd wanted to do for a long time: take his cock into her mouth and savor his essence.

She tasted and sucked, swirled her tongue over the sensitive head with a desperate abandon, an aching need to show him how much pleasure he'd given her in the last few days.

Micah's hands fisted her hair tightly, almost painfully. Glancing up, she could see that his head was back, resting against the shower stall. He looked like he was barely hanging on to his control.

She sped up her pace, sucking harder, using her hand to increase the friction and make this even more pleasurable for him.

Closing her eyes, more than ready to make him come for the first time with her mouth, Tessa was startled when Micah pulled her away from him by her hair, pulling her head back far enough that she could look up at his face.

"Up!" She could see the command on his lips as he grasped her upper arms tightly and hauled her to her feet.

She was panting, warm water flooding across her back as she looked at him anxiously. "What happened? I thought you liked—"

"I love it too damn much," he answered, opening the door to the cubicle with one hand. "I can't take any more of having my dick in that beautiful mouth of yours."

He motioned her to get out, and she reluctantly stepped onto the fluffy rug in front of the shower. She began to reach for the towel she'd left out for herself, but Micah stepped behind her and wrapped his powerful arms around her waist before she could scoop it up.

Her gaze lifted until she could see his face clearly in the large mirror over the counter, her core flooding with liquid heat as she caught his expression. His eyes were dark and filled with a desperate need that echoed in her soul. For a moment, their gazes caught and held in the reflective glass, both of them communicating without words.

Finally, Micah seemed to snap, and he moved forward, urged her legs apart with his feet, then pushed urgently on her back. His feral longing was contagious, and Tessa leaned forward and placed her palms on the bathroom vanity, her only thought getting him inside her.

Her head dropped and her back arched as she felt his fingers delving between her thighs. "Please. Don't wait," she panted, knowing she couldn't take his teasing right now.

She lifted her head as he tugged on her wet hair, knowing instinctively that he wanted to say something.

"This is exactly what I wanted to do since the moment I saw you in that bathroom in the guesthouse. I wanted to bend you over and fuck you right there in the bathroom until the ache to have you went away." Her sheath contracted as she read his words in his *voice*, a low, husky sound that she could imagine in her mind.

It was hard to believe that somebody like Micah had felt instant lust when she'd been nothing more than the cleaning lady at the Sinclair guest homes. She'd been dressed in her oldest clothing, and she'd come there from a snowstorm. That couldn't have been an enticing sight, but she believed him. Even then, she'd wanted him, too. But she'd also been staring at his nude body straight from the shower. Her attraction made sense. His . . . not so much.

"Do it now, then," Tessa begged as she met his hungry eyes. "Do it."

"I plan on it," he said, the muscle in his jaw ticking with restraint. "It's like living out a fantasy I've had for a long time."

His fingers teased her clit, then moved through her slick heat like he owned it. She moaned and let her head drop back down again, unable to speak even if she wanted to, as she felt the head of his cock finally probing the entrance to her channel.

She pushed her hips back eagerly as Micah surged forward, then she whimpered in ecstasy as he seated himself to the root.

"Yes," she cried out, her entire body quivering in anticipation.

He grasped her hips, hammering into her as she quickly caught his frenzied pace and pushed back to meet every thrust.

Micah fucked just like he lived his life: fast, furious, and like a force of nature that couldn't be stopped.

Not that Tessa *wanted* him to stop. She loved it when Micah reacted to her like this, as though she was the only thing in the world he wanted, needed. It was that very intensity that made being with him so raw, so incredibly carnal that she lost herself to the ferociously erotic reaction her body had to Micah's merciless pursuit of her orgasm.

Her climax didn't do a slow approach. It steamrolled over her as Micah sought and found her clit, fingering boldly as he pummeled into her again and again.

"Oh, God. Micah!" she screamed as her muscles clenched around his cock.

He grasped her hips harder, surging hard a few more times before he stopped, spilling his warm release deep inside her.

Her body still trembling, Tessa lifted her head to watch him. His head was tilted slightly back, the big muscles in his neck flexing, his expression ravaged as he opened his mouth in what she knew was a silent roar of triumph.

In that moment, she wished that she could hear him as he came, but she satisfied herself with watching his big, glorious body shudder, knowing that he'd had the same mind-blowing sensations that she'd experienced.

She was in his arms within moments, her exhausted, limp, and spent body being supported by Micah's strength as he lifted her ass onto the counter and cradled her head against his shoulder. Tessa sighed as his hand slid up and down her naked back, and she found a resting place for her arms around his neck.

Her mind and body relaxed, feeling Micah's chest rise and fall against her, the pace steadily decreasing as they both caught their breath.

It's like the calm after a storm.

Tessa had come to realize that, although she'd been surviving, she hadn't been living until she'd met Micah, until she'd had him to challenge her to reach higher. She'd been coasting through life, but she'd never really been happy for most of her entire adult life. Maybe when she'd been younger and skating, her ambitions had consumed her. But somewhere along the way, she'd lost who she was and what she'd wanted from life. Yeah, her life had changed irrevocably, but she'd let herself and other people set some pretty tame limits on what she could and couldn't do because she was deaf.

Now, she understood that she had very few limits unless she wanted them. Of course, there were always going to be things she couldn't do, but that was probably true for most people for one reason or another.

Hadn't her unexpected battle with meningitis taught her that life was fleeting and so very short to put things off because of fear? Maybe it hadn't back then, but she could see so much more clearly now.

She hugged Micah tighter, knowing the day would come when she'd have to let go, but she wasn't going to regret what had happened between them. Ever. The pain of letting go would never outweigh the experience of being with him, even if it only lasted a little while.

When they finally disentangled themselves, she saw a sudden worried thought pass over his expression.

"What?" she asked, reaching out to catch his arm.

"Tessa, I didn't use a condom. I didn't use a fucking condom!" Micah raked his hand through his wet hair.

Her heart dropped as she realized they'd both been so caught up in the moment that the thought of using protection hadn't even crossed their minds. Micah was upset with himself, and understandably so, but at least she could rid him of his concerns.

Tightening her hand on his arm, she said, "I was checked after I was with Rick. I'm clean of any type of disease, and right before I got sick, I got a ten-year IUD put in. I thought I was going to get married, and I wasn't planning a family anytime soon." Actually, now that she thought about it, she wasn't even sure Rick had even wanted kids. The long-term birth control had been his idea. "I didn't have it removed. I won't get pregnant. Trust me. I won't let you fall," she said softly, hoping he'd lighten up.

Micah took her by the shoulders and stared down at her. "You think I was worried about that? I want—" He stopped and started again. "I need for you to trust me, Tessa. I've never *not* used a condom, and you know it's been a while for me, but I don't do that shit. I don't *forget* to use a damn condom. It was a fucking stupid thing for me to do. I'm clean, but what if I wasn't? Jesus, Tessa! Don't ever trust a guy who is panting after you to not wear a condom."

Her mind finally cleared, understanding what he was trying to say in his convoluted explanation. She smiled as she tightened her arms around his neck. "So are you saying I shouldn't trust you? You're the only man I'm sleeping with right now."

"No. That's not what I'm saying. I was speaking generally."

She rubbed her breasts against his chest. "I'm speaking specifically," she replied. "If I'm only sleeping with you, we're both clean, and I'm on birth control, can I trust you?"

"Hell, yes, you can trust me. Do you think my dick is really going to get hard for anybody else right now? It's fucking fixated on you."

"Then trust me and try it again. I'd kind of like to finish what I started in the shower."

Her heart raced as she watched his anguished expression. She understood what he meant, that he never wanted her to trust another guy to always tell her the truth. His heavy breath wafted across her cheek as she moved closer to him and she asked, "Do you trust me?"

"You I trust. Other men . . . no, I damn well don't."

"I'm not with any other men right now."

"Thank fuck! And you never will be, so this discussion is unnecessary anyway."

His mouth crashed down on hers so fast that she never did get to ask him what he meant, and it was quickly forgotten as Micah's sensual assault to her senses made her forget that anything else but him existed.

CHAPTER 12

Later that evening, Julian ducked into Shamrock's Pub more out of necessity than because he wanted a beer. Quickly taking a rickety seat by one of the windows, he opened the threadbare curtain and looked out at Main Street, hoping to hell he'd lost his group of adoring fans.

Slumping back in the chair when he didn't see anybody coming, he pulled off his baseball cap and sunglasses, dropping them onto the table.

"Running from the police?" he heard a sarcastically sweet voice ask from the bar.

He looked up and saw Kristin minding the tavern . . . again. Was anybody else ever here except her? She already had a full-time job in Sarah's office. Why was she always here?

"Not lately. But you never know," he shot back halfheartedly, not feeling like arguing with the sharp-tongued redhead tonight.

I'd rather fuck her until she stops talking and starts screaming.

His dick was already at attention just from looking at her. Kristin embodied every physical asset that turned him on. Unlike most guys in Hollywood, the last thing he wanted was a skinny model. He liked women who enjoyed food, and he was a large man. He wanted a curvy female with some flesh on her bones and an ass that he could actually grasp while he was pummeling into her body.

Unfortunately, the woman who haunted his wet dreams obviously hated him. Maybe that was why he wanted her so badly. Not only was Kristin beautiful, but she wasn't about to drop at his feet and submit. More likely, she'd knee him in the balls and walk away. Maybe he was a masochist, but he kind of liked that about her.

"What are you looking for?" she asked curiously.

"My fan club," he answered glumly. "Can I have a beer? And no milk. I already ate."

He watched as she pulled out a frosted mug and brought him whatever they had on tap. Not that he was picky. He could tell by the lightness of the liquid in the glass that it wasn't a dark, bitter brew, which was the only kind he really didn't like.

She set the mug down in front of him, placing a napkin underneath.

"You look better," she observed, reaching out to turn his face toward her.

"I'm a fast healer," he answered flatly, letting her examine his features. Her touch was impersonal but light and soft, so he let her check him out as long as she wanted.

Unfortunately, she dropped her hand almost immediately, and he was kind of disappointed. "Not busy tonight?"

The joint was empty except for him. He seemed to be the only customer.

She shrugged and crossed her arms in front of her. "It's late, and it's after Labor Day. The town gets quiet during the off-season. You missed the crowd. There must have been six or seven people here earlier," she informed him sarcastically.

Julian smirked, amused that she could throw out those kinds of comments with a perfectly straight face.

He motioned toward the chair across from him. "Then sit. Have a beer with me."

"I don't mingle with customers."

"Bullshit. You probably know most of the people in this town."

"Okay. Maybe I just don't want to talk to *you*," she answered tartly.

He shook his head. "That's not it. It's because I kissed you the other day, and now you're uncomfortable."

"Is not," she denied emphatically.

"It was an amazing kiss, by the way," he drawled.

"Not that great. I've had better," she protested. "And if you have a fan club, why bother kissing me at all?"

"Because I didn't want to kiss anybody in my fan club," he answered, locking eyes with her. "I wanted to kiss *you*."

He watched, amused, as she opened her mouth and then snapped it shut. It was the first time she'd ever looked the least bit flustered.

She wrinkled her brow and looked at him quizzically. "Why? You have women dropping at your feet."

"Not the right kind of woman." He took a slug of beer and motioned for her to sit again.

She turned, her ponytail swaying as she made her way to the back of the bar and pulled out a chilled Diet Coke, came back to the table, and sat across from him. "I'm not really joining you. My feet hurt." She popped the lid on the can and took a long gulp of the soda. "Besides, I'm done cleaning up, and I can't lock up until you leave or it hits closing time." She hesitated before she asked, "Are you really being bothered here in town? Most people are pretty used to seeing the Sinclair brothers, and you guys have been here before. We usually mind our own business."

"Usually nobody bothers any of us. But these girls all look young," he admitted disgustedly.

"Like how young?"

He shrugged. "Probably just old enough to drink."

"And you're so old?" Kristin said teasingly as she picked up his sunglasses. "Honestly, I think wearing sunglasses at night is probably a dead giveaway that you're hiding." She shook her head sadly and picked up the hat. "And since when are you a Patriots fan? You live in California."

He snatched the cap from Kristin's hand. "I didn't just buy that. I grew up on the East Coast. I don't like California teams. I've always been a Pats fan."

She gave him a doubtful look. "Okay. But I'd definitely lose the sunglasses at night."

Julian had been trying to stay on the down low for so long that he hadn't even thought about wearing the glasses after dark. Usually, if he was going out after the sun set, it was for a work function, so it didn't matter if he was recognized. "I'll take that into consideration."

"Does it ever get old? Being famous, I mean? It has to suck not being able to go anywhere without bodyguards in a crowd." She took another sip of her soda and looked at him questioningly.

It got old really fast, and Julian had been over it almost from the start. He hadn't gotten into the business for stardom or fame. He was in it because he loved movies and telling a good story. "It's part of the job. Even if it's something I hate, there's parts of every job that people aren't going to like. If you're successful, you don't have much of a choice except to deal with it."

She looked surprised. "You really don't like having women panting after you?"

He leaned forward and put his elbows on the table. "I wouldn't say that. If *you* wanted to pant after me, I wouldn't run away," he answered in a low, husky tone. "Hell, I'd love to let you catch me."

Kristin rolled her eyes at him and snorted. "Dream on, Hotshot. I never have liked being part of a crowd of groupies."

He smirked at her, enjoying her denial. Julian actually liked Kristin. He always had. She spoke her mind, and she definitely didn't worship famous people. Honestly, he didn't think she gave a damn whether he was famous or not.

"Do you like my movies?" he asked curiously.

She didn't speak for a moment, finally answering, "I only saw your first one. But yeah, I liked it. You deserved to be awarded for it. You're an amazing actor, and you brought life into the character, made the movie seem . . . real. I haven't seen the others."

"Don't bother with the most recent one," he warned her. "But you might like the second one."

"I haven't had a chance to see it. What's wrong with the last one?"

"Not enough heart," he answered stoically. "If people like special effects, it's good. But it doesn't have much emotional substance."

"And that bothers you? It was a big-budget movie."

"That might be the problem. Too much money on bling and not enough guts in the screenplay." When he'd signed on to do the film, he'd hoped that once it was produced, it would come to life. But it hadn't turned out much different from the screenplay, which was all lights, stunts, and sound.

"Why do it if you didn't like it?" Kristin questioned.

"I guess I was hopeful that it would turn out differently. It had a huge budget, but most of it got spent on the effects. Don't get me wrong, it's a fun flick. The action is nonstop, but it's not something that will touch anybody here." He put his hand on his heart.

"Sometimes, maybe that's okay. People go to movies to escape from their lives in lots of situations. I know some people will love that. A few hours of fun on the big screen is still important. It's escapism." Kristin's tone was sincere.

Julian studied her face, realizing she was actually being honest with him, and he started to wonder if she wasn't right. He'd enjoyed doing something different. Even though he didn't see it as something that might touch people on a deep level, maybe it wasn't *always* necessary to be touched that deeply. "So sometimes it's just okay to be entertained?"

She nodded. "Yes."

"Underneath your sarcasm, you're pretty insightful, Red."

"I hate that name," she said through gritted teeth.

Julian saw a glimpse of hurt cross her beautiful face, and he was instantly regretful that he'd ruined an actual discussion between them. "I'm sorry, Kristin. I was teasing. I never meant to be mean."

She shrugged it off, but Julian could tell that he'd touched a nerve with her. Unfortunately, just as he wanted to expand on his apology, he spotted his Amesport fan club. "Shit! Here they come. How in the hell did they find me?"

Kristin shot out of her chair and grabbed his hand, tugging him across the room and then behind the bar. "Get down," she hissed as she put her elbows on the worn counter.

Julian felt ridiculous as he crouched behind the bar, but he didn't feel like interacting with a crowd of hysterical young women tonight. He'd already tried to reason with them, and they'd practically ripped his clothes from his body. They weren't polite, and they were far from reasonable.

"Ladies? Can I help you?" Kristin asked casually as the crowd of young women came through the door.

"We're looking for Julian Sinclair!" a high, excited voice exclaimed.

Kristin shook her head. "Sorry. I can't help you. And we don't chase people down like rabbits in this town. The Sinclairs are part of this community, and we respect the whole family for what they've done to help Amesport."

The same overenthusiastic woman answered. "Oh, we don't live here. We're just here to find Julian. We heard he was here. We're his biggest fans."

"If you care about him that much, then you'd let him have his privacy. I understand he's dating a woman in this town, and I don't think he'd appreciate you screwing that up for him."

There was a chorus of groans as the women were notified that he might be off the eligible-bachelor market.

"He's getting married?" another female asked in a disappointed voice.

Kristin shrugged. "He might be. Look, ladies, Julian Sinclair is just a man like any other. You don't even know him. Maybe he's not worth going crazy over. Personally, I think you have to *know* a guy to actually like him."

"But he's so hot."

"He's amazing."

"He's gorgeous."

Kristin broke into the barrage of compliments. "I've heard he can also be a real dickhead," she told the women with an enormous eye-roll. "Being handsome could never make up for that."

"Sometimes it can," one of the females whined. "But if he's off the market, I guess we should give up. We have to get back home anyway. Our parents are going to be pissed that we took off a few days at the college to drive to Amesport."

"I'm sure they won't be happy," Kristin told them ominously. "But the fewer days you miss, the easier it will be for you."

The young women left looking heartbroken. Kristin strolled over to the door as the last girl left, flipped the sign to "Closed," then turned the lock on the door.

Julian rose up and watched her as she sauntered back to the bar. "You heard I was a dickhead?" he asked, amused. "And who am I marrying here in Amesport?"

"Nobody. But you wanted them off your back. It worked. They're going home now that they think you're off the market."

Julian frowned. "Did somebody actually say they thought I was a dickhead?"

"Nope. I made that up myself. But I'm sure somebody has said it somewhere."

He laughed because he couldn't stop himself. Kristin was about the crankiest woman he'd ever met, but he liked her style. No bullshit. No pretension. As he recovered, he admitted, "I owe you. Thanks."

"Don't think I won't collect," she warned him. "It's not like you're even a friend."

Still smiling, he strode over to his table. He put his sunglasses on the visor of his cap and jammed it back on his head. "I look forward to you collecting, Kristin. Anything you want is yours. You were amazing—except maybe for the dickhead part."

He walked over to the door, unlocked it, and then cracked it open. "But you're very right about one thing." He turned and looked at her, not missing the fact that she looked flushed.

She put her hands on her hips. "And what's that?"

His gaze roamed hungrily over her flame-colored hair, her soft skin, and her curvaceous body as he answered mysteriously, "I am definitely just a man."

There was no answer, and Julian didn't expect one as he walked through the door and closed it softly behind him.

CHAPTER 13

"Xander overdosed. He's in the hospital," Julian informed Micah as he arrived back at the guesthouse.

Having just dropped back in to the guesthouse for a few minutes to get some stuff this morning, Micah had been certain he'd be back to Tessa before she woke up. Obviously, that wasn't going to happen now.

He looked at his brother, dressed casually in jeans and a T-shirt just like him, Julian's usual humor totally absent from his expression.

"When? How bad is he?" It wasn't the first time it had happened, but every time, Micah hoped it would never happen again.

"He'll live, but he'll need to stay a few days in the hospital. They want him to be discharged to rehab. They tried to call you, but they couldn't reach you. They got to me through my publicist."

"Damn! I just got a new phone, and I asked for a new number. I killed my old phone during a climb with Tessa. My executives don't even have it yet. Tessa is the only one who has the new one. I should have been pickier about who I gave it out to over the years. I was getting calls from people I don't even remember."

"What do you think about rehab? I think he might need it," Julian said huskily.

Micah took a deep breath, knowing it was time to clue his middle brother in on a few things. "He's gone the rehab route, and it isn't his first overdose. He checks out of rehab the minute he's allowed to go, and he won't talk to anybody about getting help. Something's going on with him, Julian, but I have no idea how to get through to him," Micah rasped in a frustrated voice.

"Why didn't you say something?"

"I wanted you to have your time. These are your moments, everything you've worked for in the past decade," Micah answered in a low tone.

"But Xander's my *brother*," Julian argued. "If he's in trouble, I want to help."

Micah exploded. "Don't you think I haven't fucking tried? I'm probably in California once a week, but I have a company to run, and Xander isn't doing a damn thing to help himself. He's addicted to prescription narcotics, the same drugs he used to keep his pain stable right after the murders. He drinks his hard alcohol straight from the bottle, uses it to wash down the pills until he's unconscious. He doesn't want help, Julian. I've tried."

"Then he needs to try again or he's going to die," Julian barked.

"If he goes to rehab, he just leaves within a few days. The doctors say he has to want to kick the substance abuse. I don't know what happened to him, but there's more haunting him than he's ever admitted. I know he watched Mom and Dad die right before his eyes, but it's more than that. He's scarred inside and out." Feeling defeated, Micah turned away from Julian to go pack his bag. "I'll go. I'll see what I can do."

Micah stumbled as his vision filled with an ominous aura of color, and he automatically slapped his hand on the back of his neck.

Shit! Not now. This couldn't happen right now.

Julian was next to Micah as he froze before entering the hallway.

"Hey, bro, you okay? What's wrong? Damn, you're as white as a sheet." Julian put his hand under Micah's bicep. "You almost fell."

"I saw colors. I'm going to go lie down for a little while," Micah admitted hoarsely, knowing he didn't have long to explain.

"The migraines are back?" Julian said anxiously. "I thought you outgrew them. I thought you hadn't experienced them in years."

"I thought so, too," Micah grumbled. "They started again not long ago. I came here because the doctor suggested some downtime. My executives are handling the business right now."

"You're not eating right, not taking care of yourself, and you're babysitting our baby brother, aren't you?" Julian said angrily as he steered Micah toward the bedroom his brother had been using in the guesthouse. "Do you have pills?"

"Yeah. They help some. I'll sleep on the way to California."

Julian followed him. "You're not going. Get your ass in a dark place and I'll go deal with Xander. Looks like it's my turn. Has it been that bad? Be straight with me, Micah."

"Yeah. It's that bad. This is his third overdose, and most of the time he won't answer messages. I have to go there to see if he's okay. He's usually drunk and high as a kite on drugs. We need to cut off his source. The docs aren't giving them to him, but he's getting them somehow." Micah collapsed on the bed, a dull ache starting behind his eye and shooting through the side of his head.

Julian looked at the prescription bottle at the side of Micah's bed before shaking out the tablets while going to get water from the bathroom. He returned and handed Micah the pills and a glass of water.

Julian made a few calls to arrange his transportation to California, then told Micah, "I'll be tempted to kick Xander's ass, but I want to understand why he's doing this. He was always the nicest out of the three of us. He didn't drink much, and he sure as hell didn't do drugs. What the fuck happened to him?"

"Bring him here," Micah demanded. "He needs a different scene. I don't know if he'll agree, but try."

"I'll do more than try. I'll drag his ass back here whether he likes it or not."

"Be careful. He bites now," Micah warned, knowing Xander was beyond surly.

"Then I'll fucking bite him back," Julian growled. "I'm sorry I have to go, Micah. I know you'll be miserable. Anything else you need?"

"Text Tessa for me. Her cell is in my phone. I can't be with her today. Maybe tomorrow." Gritting his teeth at the intense pain that shot through the right side of his head, Micah tried to stay aware of his surroundings and function a little longer.

"Call me as soon as you can," Julian said quietly and left the room, closing the door quietly behind him.

Micah buried his head under the pillow, knowing Julian would take care of things. As kids, his brothers had seen him go through this many times. Julian knew he'd be back to normal in a day or two.

As he finally gave in to the pain, Micah hoped that Julian could get through to Xander, do what he himself had failed to do: straighten Xander's ass out for good.

⌒～⌒

Tessa was getting her morning coffee when she noticed she had a text from Micah. For some reason, he must have left early this morning and hadn't returned yet.

She used a finger to open the text as she took her first sip of coffee.

Micah: Now isn't a good time to be with you. Maybe in the future. I'm sorry.

After reading it three times, she still didn't know what to make of the message. Obviously, he'd decided to back off, and even though she'd told herself she wouldn't be sad when he left, her heart shattered.

I knew it wasn't forever. I knew he'd have to go.

As she glanced out the window, the sight of a plane taking off from the airport was the final stab to her heart. Amesport didn't do commercial flights, so it had to be a private plane, and there weren't many of those in her town. In fact, the airport had been pretty much closed until Grady Sinclair had decided to make his permanent home in Amesport and brought his big private jet along with him. Eventually, the rest of the brothers had moved here, and private aircraft came along with them, too.

Most people in Amesport knew when a Sinclair was leaving or returning, since they were about the only ones who really used the airstrip outside of town.

Tessa finished her coffee, trying not to shed a tear. Keeping with her routine, she did her morning run and then headed to the arena. She ran through her routine several times, but her heart ached that, for once, Micah wasn't there on the sidelines to cheer her on or let her know if she was off time with her music with the silly little gestures they'd made up for each scenario.

She didn't arrive home until dinnertime, and the house seemed eerily empty. It was her fault. She'd allowed herself to get way too attached to Micah, and everything seemed grim without him here to laugh with her, talk to her, touch her, and make her feel like she was part of a couple instead of terribly alone and isolated.

As she tossed a frozen dinner in the microwave, she noticed that a message had popped up on her phone again, but she didn't recognize the number.

Did you get my message this morning?

The only text she'd gotten was from Micah, and this number wasn't his. She typed back cautiously.

Who is this?

It took a few minutes for the sender to reply.

Julian Sinclair. I don't think Micah wanted me to tell you anything, but he hasn't called me and I'm getting a little worried. My cousins are all off the Peninsula today, and I need somebody to check on Micah. I don't suppose you're near that area right now?

Micah? He was still here?

Where was *Julian*? Where was *Micah*? The two of them texted back and forth for a few minutes before she got the information she needed. Micah was at Jared's guesthouse, sick. Julian was in California because Xander had overdosed, and it had been a hurried text from Julian that she'd gotten this morning from Micah's phone. Julian had scribbled down her number in case he needed it, utilizing her now because none of his relatives were available.

It hadn't been *Micah* blowing her off. It had been *Julian* trying to tell her that Micah had to stay home with a migraine headache, that he couldn't make it back to her today.

Her fingers flew as she texted back to Julian again.

I'll go. How is Xander?

She got a response a few moments later.

X is ornery as hell, but okay for now. Thanks for checking. Micah never has asked for help when he needed it. But I'd feel better if somebody was there. His migraines can get pretty bad.

Tessa gathered her things, wanting to get to the Peninsula as soon as possible.

I'm on my way. I'll take care of Micah. I promise.

Julian sent his thanks, and a vow to let her know any new information on Xander when he got it. She stuffed her phone in her purse and made her little economy vehicle get to the Peninsula as quickly as possible, driving faster than she'd gone even as a lead-footed teenager, in an effort to get to Micah.

The door was locked when she reached Jared's guesthouse, but she had a key, and she felt no remorse for using it when she wasn't working. Since darkness was beginning to fall, she flipped on some lights in the living room and kitchen, getting a glass of ice water, a cool cloth, and some crackers from the cupboard before creeping quietly to the door of the bedroom where Micah slept.

She knew the house, knew what bedroom Micah had used when he stayed here. She cleaned these houses, and she was familiar with all of the guest homes.

Cautiously, she pushed open the door, seeing Micah on the bed moving restlessly. She went and pulled the curtains as tightly closed as possible, feeling guilty that she hadn't been there before dusk to try to help him. Once the remaining sunlight was completely blocked, she put the items she'd gathered on the bedside table and lightly put her hand on Micah's forehead.

His skin was wet and clammy, his body covered in sweat. Slowly, she lowered the pillow from his head and placed the cool cloth across his forehead.

Micah startled and turned on the dim bedside lamp on his nightstand.

"Tessa?" he hissed in a low voice, his eyes puffy and red as he looked at her, seeming confused.

"Yes," she whispered quietly. "Lie still. Do you need more medication?"

"Yeah. I couldn't get up to take it. I think Julian left it in the bathroom."

"Are you nauseous?"

"No. Not anymore."

She got up and went into the small half bath, closing the door before she flipped on the light and found his pills. Shaking out a dose and replacing the cap, she went back to his bedside and helped him take the pills with the cold water she'd brought in with her.

After feeding him a few crackers, she went and got a basin of cold water so she could periodically change the cool compress. Kicking off her shoes, she lay gently beside him.

"How did you know?" Micah said weakly.

"Julian. He was worried," she shared in a whisper, knowing that noises were going to bother him.

"I didn't want you to see me like this," he rumbled.

"I want to be here if you need me," she answered. "Just rest now. I'll be right here beside you if you want anything."

Careful not to touch him, she reached across his body and cut off the light, effectively ending any conversation since she couldn't see him.

He reached out and wrapped an arm around her waist, bodily pulling her closer, and she rested a hand cautiously on his chest. She wasn't sure if he wanted to be touched.

Apparently, he wanted to feel her, to be touched by her. He fell asleep soon after she'd turned off the light, his body less restless as he reached up his free hand and covered the one she had laid on his chest.

CHAPTER 14

⌒

Micah awoke in a dark room, disoriented because he couldn't remember exactly where he was, but the warmth of Tessa's hand in his calmed him down, forcing him to think.

Xander.

The migraine.

The fucking pain.

Then, Tessa had come. She'd cared for him, but most of the details were fuzzy.

Slowly, he remembered that Julian had gone to California because Xander had overdosed. He wasn't sure why or how Tessa had known he needed her, but Julian had to be the source of that information. He was the only one who knew. As his brain started to clear, he vaguely remembered Tessa telling him that Julian had texted her because he'd been worried about Micah.

The excruciating pain was gone, leaving only a dull ache, a minor discomfort that Micah knew would wear off during the next few hours. He shifted and looked at the lighted bedside clock, realizing he'd been incoherent for almost twenty-four hours. The duration was shorter than his last episode, which had gone on for two days.

He knew it was morning, well beyond daylight, but the curtains were carefully pulled across the large windows in the room, leaving it nearly completely dark.

"Micah? Are you okay?" Tessa vaulted into a sitting position, immediately awake.

His chest ached just from hearing the concern in her voice, the genuine fear for his health. Reaching back, he turned on the light so he could communicate with her, sitting up slowly.

Taking her frightened face between his hands, he said, "I'm fine. Sleep, Tessa. I know you probably didn't get much rest." He could tell by the way she'd reacted the moment he moved that she'd slept lightly. She was still dressed in a pair of jeans and a T-shirt, apparently acting as his guardian angel as he slept.

She yawned as she replied, "I slept. You conked out after you took your pills and ate some crackers. How are you feeling?"

"Better," he said uncomfortably, not completely at ease with being helpless and in pain with anybody watching. "You didn't need to come over."

"Maybe not. But I wanted to," she told him softly, lifting a hand to his face to stroke his whiskered jaw. "My mom used to suffer with migraines. I know how bad it can be."

Micah thought about how she'd probably pulled the curtains closed, fetched cold compresses, and sought out his pills the night before. He always had found his migraines emasculating. The condition was a lot more common in women than men, and he'd always wondered why it had to happen to him. As a teenager, he'd felt like a wuss when he had to discontinue his activities because he had a stupid headache. Since he always had warning, very few of his friends even knew about his condition. The only ones who had ever understood were his brothers and his parents.

"This one didn't last as long as the last one. Maybe they'll eventually go away," he grumbled.

"Is that what happened? They went away and then came back?"

"Yeah. Until the last year or so, I hadn't had one in over a decade."

"After your parents were killed and Xander was injured. That's why your doctor wanted you to get away from all your stresses?"

Micah shrugged. "Pretty much. He thought maybe it was happening again because of the way my parents died, the situation with Xander, and the lifestyle change since I started my own business."

Tessa nodded. "He's probably right. My mom's migraines only happened when she was under a lot of stress. After my dad died, she had them a lot."

"I can't just give up my life. I escaped for a while, but I have to live in reality. I love my company, and I love my brother," he told her angrily.

Tessa didn't let his hostile expression bother her. She knew Micah was angry at the situation and not at her. "I know you do, but that doesn't mean you have to shoulder all of the burdens in your family. Did Julian give you a hassle about taking care of Xander this time?"

Micah thought for a minute before answering, "No. I think he was pissed because I didn't tell him everything."

"You should have told him. I know how it feels when one sibling sacrifices so much for another. Julian deserved to know so he could help. Maybe he'd have chosen to share the burden."

"He would have. That's the problem," Micah answered huskily.

Tessa rested her hand on his shoulder. "It doesn't have to be a problem. If you shared the situation, I know that your cousins would help, too. Maybe Xander needs a major intervention with as much backup as you can get."

"He does. And I think that's probably going to happen. Julian swears he's bringing Xander back here so he can get away from his sources in California."

"Good. We can arrange for an expert to be there to help. Now let me get you some breakfast. You must be starving."

Micah narrowed his eyes as he looked at Tessa. He wanted to reach out, scoop her up, and then bury himself inside her, forget for a short time about everything except her. She was beautifully mussed up from sleep, and her spiraled curls were wild and pretty damn sexy. There was only one thing that stopped him.

"Christ! I stink. How did you manage to stay in the same room with me, much less the same bed?" The fact that he could smell his own sweat told him that his stench was beyond a smell that she could get used to or go nose-blind to.

Tessa smiled at him. "It's not like I haven't smelled your sweat before."

His cock stiffened as Micah thought of the many times he'd worked up a sweat in bed with her, but this was different. "It's stale sweat, and it stinks." He always perspired heavily when he was going through one of his painful episodes, but he was usually alone.

"Go shower and I'll strip the bed," she demanded as she got out of the bed. "It's really not *that* bad. Are you going to be okay by yourself?"

Micah was tempted to tell her that he wouldn't be all right, and he needed her naked and in the shower with him. However, he refused to put her through inhaling any more of his pungent body odor. "I'm good."

She was already pulling the sheets off the bed as he exited the bedroom, and Micah's chest ached once again at the thought that Tessa had stayed with him, even though it hadn't been the least bit pleasant.

He wasn't used to that, having somebody care for him, and he wasn't sure he was completely comfortable with it. But damn, it felt good knowing that Tessa had his back.

I'll be right here beside you if you need me.

Tessa's soft declaration the night before drifted through his mind as he quickly stripped out of his disgusting-smelling clothing. He hadn't imagined them. Her words had been real. And she'd stayed there for him all night long.

"I need her. I do fucking need her, and not just for my migraines," he growled as he flipped on the water.

Tessa connected with him on a level that was almost terrifying for a man like him. He was used to being the oldest, the problem solver in his immediate family. When his parents had been murdered, he'd handled everything, taken care of everything. He was used to being the caretaker, and he wasn't quite certain what to do with a woman who actually cared about him, saw who he was beyond his money.

Keep her!

"Mine," he rasped as he stepped into the hot shower. "She's mine."

He wasn't sure how he could work everything out, and he didn't have a plan. For once, he was going by gut reaction, primal instinct, and a certainty that he felt clear down to his soul.

Tessa Sullivan was his, and he was *never* going to let her go.

Micah felt more human as he sat at the kitchen table and drank a cup of coffee. Tessa had put the sheets into the wash and then decided to go take a shower herself before fixing breakfast.

He nearly choked on his coffee as Tessa strolled out to the kitchen fresh from the shower, her damp ringlets of blonde hair barely tamed, and her gorgeous legs exposed because she'd pulled on one of his button-down shirts. It was way too big for her, and the sleeves were rolled up to her elbows, the hem of the shirt hitting her at about midthigh. But seeing her in something that belonged to him had his cock straining against his jeans almost immediately.

"Nice shirt," he choked out as she looked at him.

"I hope you don't mind. I came right here. I didn't bring anything clean."

Her face was contrite, and he fucking hated that. Hell, Tessa could feel free to wear every shirt in his closet if she wanted. In fact, she could do anything she liked as long as she stayed with him. "Keep it. It looks better on you than it did on me," he rasped, dirty thoughts filling his mind as he wondered if she was wearing underwear, since she hadn't brought any extra. "Did you borrow my boxers, too?"

She flushed as she stopped at the table and looked down at him. "All of my clothes are in the washer."

The adorably flustered look on her face sent Micah over the edge. Jesus, she was irresistible when she wasn't sure what to say, which didn't happen very often.

He picked up his empty mug and dropped it on a small, decorative table behind him before he stood and hoisted her onto the table to sit in front of him. "I think I need to investigate exactly what you're wearing underneath that shirt."

"Nothing," she admitted, her gaze fixed on his mouth. "I already told you that."

He put his hands on her thighs and slowly slid them upward, edging the shirt higher. "I want to look."

"I thought you were hungry," she replied in a tremulous, aroused voice.

"I am. That's why I want to see my breakfast, baby," he answered hoarsely, releasing an enormous breath as the shirt went up to her waist and he saw her bare pussy. He pushed her body down on the table and jerked the material until every button popped, revealing Tessa in all of her naked glory, spread out on the table for him like a fucking buffet.

"God, you're beautiful," he told her reverently as she continued to stare at his lips in her supine position.

"I feel beautiful when you look at me," she answered in a breathy, needy voice. "I've never felt that way before."

Micah was both irritated and relieved that no other man had told her just how breathtaking she was. She should know. She should realize that just the sight of her could make a guy lose his mind.

He bent over and kissed her, a slow sensual embrace that allowed him to explore her mouth thoroughly, completely, tenderly. For once, he didn't want to rush to possess her. Not that the urge wasn't there, but his need to worship and pleasure her was even greater right now.

His mouth moved up her neck before his tongue started exploring the soft skin of her ear. Her whimper of pleasure was like beautiful music to his ears, and he moved lower to take one of her perfect nipples into his mouth. His lips moved over her creamy flesh, then focused on nipping and sucking the pebbled tips into hard peaks, one after the other.

She whined disappointedly as he moved lower, so he took her hands and placed them on her breasts, encouraging her without words to keep pleasuring her breasts. It took her a few awkward moments, but as he parted her thighs and began to tease her slick folds with his fingers, her movements became urgent, her fingers plucking at her breasts as she released a loud moan.

"Please, Micah. Please."

God, he loved hearing his name come from her lips, loved hearing her beg him to finish her off. But he wasn't ready to make her come. When it happened, he wanted to see her come apart with his mouth all over her. She was his to taste, to explore, and he planned on making this the best she'd ever had.

His tongue slid down her tight belly, and the fragrant aroma of her desire hit him hard in the gut, made him salivate to taste her. Knowing he couldn't wait any longer, he used his fingers to part her folds, exposing her throbbing clit and pink sweetness to his gaze. The flesh there glistened with moisture, begging him to indulge in what he already knew was the sweetest nectar he'd ever had.

He dove in with one long lick from bottom to top, lingering on the tiny bundle of nerves as he began to devour her.

"Oh, Micah. Yes. Please."

Her voice was pleading and quivering with arousal, and he intensified his efforts, burying his face in her pussy and letting himself drown in her pleasure. He licked every luxurious drop of her arousal he could find, satisfied that every bit of that dew was because she wanted him. That knowledge pleased him on a level he'd never experienced before.

He groaned into her flesh, finally catching her clit with his teeth lightly, then flicking it mercilessly with his tongue. Stroking the sensitive flesh of her inner thighs as he continued to consume her, he could feel her legs trembling as her moans grew incoherent and wild.

I like her just like this: uninhibited and so turned on that she can't think of anything except needing me to make her come.

He growled into her flesh as her hands speared into his hair, gripping his locks so tightly that he knew she was going to have to let go.

"Micah! Make. Me. Come!"

He smiled into her wet pussy, amused by how she went from pleading to demanding. But he wasn't about to deny her. He doubted he could refuse this woman much of anything now that she'd practically taken up residence in his soul.

He increased the pressure on the engorged nub that he knew needed stimulation, grinding his tongue against her until her entire body began to shudder and she arched her back. Her hands tightened in his hair painfully, but he wasn't complaining. He plunged two fingers into her silky sheath, wanting to feel her grip his fingers as volatile spasms rocked her body.

"Micah!" she screamed without inhibitions, her pleasure vibrating throughout her voice.

He lapped at her juices as she spilled more when she climaxed violently, until her grip on his hair relaxed and he could hear her panting for breath.

He pulled her limp body into a sitting position and cradled her against his chest, his arms tightening around her, sheltering her in her moment of vulnerability.

They stayed just like that until Tessa recovered her breath, then she pulled back and sent him a mock frown. "I was supposed to be getting you breakfast. Maybe I should have put on your boxers."

He smirked at her. "I ate. Breakfast was delicious. And I think underwear is highly overrated. Believe me, once I saw you in my shirt, nothing was going to stop me from having you for a meal."

"You need food," she admonished him.

"I need you," he corrected.

She lifted a hand and stroked it lightly through his hair. "I need you, too. So much it's scary sometimes. Julian sent a really quick text from your phone just saying that it wasn't a good time to be seeing me, but maybe he could in the future. And he said he was sorry. I saw the jet, so I thought you left." Her eyes glistened with moisture as she added, "Don't ever do that to me, okay? I know this isn't forever, but please come and say good-bye. Promise me."

"I'll fucking kill him," Micah rumbled. "I just meant for him to let you know I couldn't do our run and that I was sorry."

Tessa shook her head. "It wasn't his fault. He was in a hurry and worried about Xander. I understand. But I felt how much it would hurt if you just went without saying good-bye. So don't, okay? You've become my lover, but also a friend. I can handle good-bye, but not a brush-off."

He was irritated as he grasped her chin and tilted her face up to him. "Hey, when I said I'd never let you fall, I meant it. I'll never brush you off, Tessa. Never." As he looked into her beautiful eyes, he added, "And I'm still going to kill Julian."

"No, you won't," she said calmly.

He hurt you, and that's unacceptable to me. "I might," he argued.

Micah knew there would never be a permanent good-bye for him and Tessa. Just like Beatrice had predicted, Tessa was the only woman for him. He might be hardheaded, but he wasn't stupid. Somehow, he'd find a way to make her his for the rest of their lives.

"Breakfast?" she murmured.

She was worried about feeding him, and he was worried about keeping her forever. Somehow that seemed ironic, since he was usually the one who was thinking about changing the subject when a woman tried to get into heavier things. Maybe it was some kind of fucked-up karma that he'd finally found a woman he couldn't live without, and all she wanted was to make him breakfast.

He let go of her reluctantly and helped her off the table. "I'll call Julian."

Tessa cupped his cheek. "Everything will be all right, Micah. Xander will find his way back to us. He was a good guy. That man is still there. I think Xander just needs to find himself again."

He took her hand and kissed her lightly on the forehead, aching to take her back to bed and lose himself inside her. "I don't suppose you'd like a nap first?" he asked suggestively.

"Absolutely not. You're still recovering. You should have eaten by now. I'm already beating myself up because I let you . . . you know . . ." She let out a disgusted sigh.

Then, she turned on her heel and headed for the kitchen. Micah was not the least bit surprised that she was worried more about him than indulging in a morning session of bliss that he knew they both enjoyed. Because that was his Tessa, and he couldn't help but grin as he watched her try to keep his shirt closed—a garment that was now minus the buttons—as she started on breakfast.

CHAPTER 15

Later that afternoon, Tessa smiled as she picked up the buttons of Micah's shirt from the floor. Jared's wife, Mara, had kindly loaned her a pair of yoga pants and a shirt that she said were too small for her anyway, and had left the guesthouse a short time later with a look that told Tessa she definitely wanted to know the scoop on her and Micah being shacked up together. But Mara had been too polite to ask.

She took the buttons and set them on the kitchen table along with the clean shirt that she'd washed, refusing to throw it away. She'd put the buttons back on, and if Micah didn't want it, she'd keep it. Or maybe she just wouldn't ask him. He'd said she could have it. The shirt had good memories, and that would eventually be all she had of her time with Micah Sinclair.

She turned to see the guesthouse door open and Micah coming through. He looked well recovered from his migraine, and almost boyishly excited.

As she looked and saw the dog he was crooning to at his side, her jaw dropped in surprise. She didn't know that he *had* a dog, much less one that looked like it belonged to a questionable pedigree. In easier terms, she'd say he was a mutt, maybe with some Border collie and

Labrador. The canine was adorable, though, with floppy ears and an intelligent stance as he sat and looked up at Micah with something akin to hero worship.

"I didn't know you had a dog," Tessa said excitedly as she approached dog and man. "Is it friendly?"

Micah grinned at her and handed her the leash. "For you, *he* definitely will be. He's yours."

She shook her head in denial, but at the same time dropped to her knees and sunk her fingers into the dog's silky coat. "He's adorable." She wasn't lying. The animal might be mixed breed, but his brown-and-white coat was well groomed, and when his dark eyes turned attentively to her, she smiled. "I've always wanted a dog, but I always traveled too much when I was younger. When I got older, I was so busy that it didn't seem fair to leave an animal home alone so much." She glanced up at Micah with tear-filled eyes. "I'd love to have him, but I don't know if I can."

"You won't have to leave him alone." Micah held out a scrap of material to her. "Homer is a service dog. A certified hearing dog, to be exact."

Tessa grabbed the cloth and noticed that it was a dog jacket that was stamped with "Service Dog" on the side.

"Homer?" she asked, still stunned by what was happening.

"He was a rescue dog. Apparently, he wasn't treated well as a pup, but he's so smart that they were able to train him. The staff thought all he wanted was a good home, so they named him Homer."

Tessa's eyes dropped from Micah's face to the dog she was unconsciously stroking. "Poor guy," she crooned as the dog sat at attention, as though he was waiting for a command. "What does a hearing dog do?"

"I think Homer just wants affection. He'll do most anything for you. If there's somebody at the door, he'll get your attention and let you know. He'll warn you about any dangerous noises. Hell, he'll even be your alarm clock if you set an alarm, and get you up when it goes off. He's a pretty capable mutt."

A lone tear fell from her eye, and the dog immediately licked it from her cheek.

"I didn't know hearing dogs even existed. They provide ears to deaf people?"

"They do," Micah responded. "There are organizations that take in rescue dogs and train them. I was lucky enough to get Homer. The person who wanted him backed out, and they called to tell me I could take him since I was on the waiting list. He just got here this morning in my private jet. They sent him with a trainer, and she helped me put him through his routine and training so I could teach you. Watch this."

Tessa kept stroking the dog's head as Micah stepped out the door. After a few minutes, he knocked.

Homer was immediately at attention, pawing her first and then running to the door over and over again until she got up and let Micah in. Instinctively, she patted the dog's side and muttered, "Good boy."

The canine looked up at her adoringly and Tessa's heart melted. "I think he likes me." Her eyes shifted to Micah.

"I talked about you all the way back to the house. I think he knows who he belongs to. He's energetic and young, so he can do your runs with you. Hell, put his service jacket on and there's almost nowhere he can't go. He can even come to New York with you."

"I can't believe you did this. Why?"

Micah shrugged. "You said you didn't want to try the implants again, and I thought Homer would be useful."

"You don't care if I don't hear?" The question didn't come out the way she'd wanted to ask it. What she'd meant was, didn't it matter to him that she was deaf and chose to stay that way?

"I want you to do whatever makes you happy, Tessa."

Tears started spilling from her eyes as she realized that Micah really *didn't* care if she wasn't willing to do the implants again to regain her hearing, as long as she was happy with whatever decision she made. "I might try again someday," she admitted. "I've been afraid, and I can't keep using money as an excuse."

"You have funds. Liam told me. Why haven't you ever looked at your money?"

"I don't know. Maybe I was afraid that if I knew exactly what I had, I wouldn't have any excuses anymore."

"Liam has plenty of money to refurbish the restaurant. He just needs time."

She nodded. "I know. But I like to keep busy or I go stir-crazy. Plus, I want to make money of my own. I guess I've always been able to rationalize that the money was Liam's, and I really didn't know what he had. He put what he insists is my money into my personal bank account for me a few days ago. He deposited my share of our inheritance, and my profits from the restaurant. I haven't looked at what I have. I live off what I make in tips and working other jobs. I really wanted *him* to take the money Mom and Dad left, and the profits on the restaurant. He does a lot there, and he gave up a lot for me."

"I don't think he regrets his life. He's still consulting on some movies, and he seems to like being at the restaurant."

Tessa's expression registered surprise. "He still does work on movies?"

"You didn't know?"

She'd never really asked. Maybe she needed to spend more time with Liam, asking questions. "No. I didn't know. God, he worries about me so much that he doesn't even date."

"I have a feeling that's his choice. He seems to have his eye on one of his employees."

"How do you know that? Who?" God, she'd love it if Liam finally found himself a woman that he cared about and who recognized how caring he really was. She'd tried to set him up with friends several times, but it had never worked out.

"I only saw her briefly, but Liam couldn't seem to take his eyes off her. She's pretty—long, dark hair—and young."

"I know who you're talking about. She's new, and she hasn't been at the restaurant for long. She isn't *that* young."

"Tell Liam that. He seems to be pining for a woman that he'll never approach. And the feelings look mutual." He paused before adding, "Do you want to see what Homer can do?"

"Yes. Very much." She knew without a doubt she was going to keep this dog, but . . . "I'm sure you paid for him. I want to pay you back." She almost flinched at the brooding look on Micah's face as she spoke.

"Homer is a gift. And I think I got him for selfish reasons. I want you to have protection and help if you need it." His face was unreadable.

"Thank you," she said simply, knowing there was no way Micah was going to take payment.

She watched as he put Homer through his paces, doing different things to make the dog alert her. Any noise seemed to trigger his response to make her acknowledge it, and the more she praised him, the more he responded to her. Her dog was also trained in obedience, and he responded to those commands perfectly.

When he finished, Micah remarked, "You'll bond with him, and he'll bond with you. Eventually, you're the only one he'll respond to."

She broke the "stay" command that she'd given him, causing Homer to wander over to get some affection. She gave it to him willingly, scratching the dog's belly as he rolled over to get more attention.

"He's so cute," Tessa crooned as the dog sat up again and stayed in a sitting position by her side.

"He's well trained. He can find things for you if he's familiar with the object. You can practice by showing him different items and then having him go find it."

"I could get very lazy," she said jokingly. "I assume he's potty trained."

"Of course. You can let him out, but he'll do his business and come right back. He knows his job is to watch out for you."

She rose and threw herself into his arms. "Thank you. This is the best gift I've ever received."

He closed his arms around her. "If that's what I get, I think I need to buy you a few more dogs."

Tessa snorted. "One is enough."

He took her gently by the shoulders and kissed her on the forehead so she could look at him. "He certainly came at the perfect time," Micah said, his expression grim. "I talked to one of my executives today. I forgot to call them with my new phone number. They need me in New York. I need to approve a design within the next twenty-four hours or we lose time in production. We won't meet our launch date."

Her heart fell at the idea of Micah leaving Amesport, but she smiled at him. "Then you have to go. I guess sometimes I forget that you have some pretty heavy responsibilities."

"My top people do things very well. It's me who insists on having the final inspection on any product with my company name on it before it goes to production."

She lifted an eyebrow. "A little bit anal, are you?"

"A lot when it comes to safety of a product," he admitted. "That's why I started the company. I knew extreme sports would always be risky, but safer with the right equipment."

Tessa's heart swelled with pride as she reached up a hand to stroke back that crazy lock of hair of his that was constantly out of place. Micah wasn't in business just for money; he cared about what he was manufacturing. His sole purpose was to make extreme sports as safe as possible. In Tessa's mind, there was nothing more admirable than being able to possibly save lives with better products.

"Do you need help getting ready to go?" she offered.

"Don't be so happy about getting rid of me." He glared at her unhappily. "But I'll only be gone for a day or two. I'll return in plenty of time to get some final practices in and take you to your performance."

"I'll miss you," she confessed, unable to stop the words from leaving her lips.

He grinned at her. "Good. I want you to miss me, because I know I'll miss you."

"Mara invited me to dinner with her. I guess the girls decided to do Chinese food tonight instead of Brew Magic, for a change. Emily, Sarah, and Kristin will be there, too. Hope and Jason are out of town and so are Randi and Evan, so it won't be as many women as usual. I guess I might go ahead and go."

"You could have gone even if I was here," Micah told her.

"I know," she remarked simply, bowing her head to avoid looking at him.

He grasped her chin and turned her head up again. "Hey, what is it? Something wrong?"

She shrugged. "I've always wanted to go with them, and Randi has invited me to their *female-only* lunches before, but I'm afraid it would be awkward."

He frowned. "Why?"

"I read lips, Micah. There's no way I can keep up with a group conversation now. I'd feel out of place." She could manage with one or two people, and if she was in a crowd, she could choose who to focus on. But if several people were talking at the same time, she'd probably be lost. Randi was the only one who knew ASL, and she wasn't even going to be there.

"You're intimidated by a girls' get-together?" Micah asked, looking astonished.

She lifted her chin higher. "Yes. It's daunting for a deaf woman."

She watched as Micah started to laugh. Although she couldn't hear him, she could certainly visualize his amusement.

"Stop! It's not funny!" She'd just shared one of her deepest fears, and he was *laughing*?

He grasped her shoulders again, still grinning. "Tessa, you're willing to go out in front of millions of people and skate, but you're afraid of a few women? And very nice women at that."

"You don't understand," she said glumly.

"I do. I know those fears are very real to you. But you have no reason to feel awkward. You focus on what you want to understand, and ignore the rest. You won't feel awkward or lost. These women want to be your friends. More than likely, they want to know what your relationship is with me. Don't listen to a thing they say about me."

His words made her smile just a little. "It's awfully arrogant to think that all they want to do is talk about the men in their lives. Sarah is a physician with a remarkable IQ. Kristin is a medical professional. Mara is a successful businesswoman. And Emily is a business manager. Don't you think they have a lot more to talk about than men?"

"Nope."

Tessa rolled her eyes at him. "I'm sure they do," she replied adamantly. "Now do you want my help packing or not?"

"No reason to pack," Micah answered. "I have everything I need at home and on my jet. But I could use your help in the bedroom."

Tessa saw the heated look in his eyes, knowing exactly what he wanted.

"Why?" She shot him an innocent look.

"Come with me and I'll show you." He held out his hand.

His expression was both mischievous and passionate, his eyes beckoning.

Tessa couldn't have refused even if she wanted to, which she didn't. Even if it was only for a few days, she wouldn't be seeing him or feeling him for a while.

She reached out and let him take her hand.

CHAPTER 16

"So we all have to know. Are you banging Micah or what?"

Tessa thought it was strange that although her world was silent, she could almost imagine the voices of all of the women around the table trying to talk at once. The question had come from Mara, and her friend had tapped her arm before she spoke so Tessa could look at her. It had been that way with all of the women tonight, each of them tapping her forearm if they had a question for her or something they wanted to tell her. Way different from what she'd feared, Tessa found she was actually enjoying the boisterous table of females and their nonstop chatter. It wasn't awkward at all because the women were savvy enough to signal her discreetly so she wasn't excluded from the conversation.

Tessa didn't catch everything, but she was part of the conversation.

Every set of female eyes at the table was looking at her expectantly, curiously. Although she knew they were interested and teasing, Mara's question put her in a difficult situation.

She opened her mouth to speak, and then closed it, not knowing what to say.

Happily, she was saved when Homer got up from his place beside her on the floor and put his muzzle on her purse and laid a paw on her thigh. It was obviously a sign that her phone was buzzing.

"Excuse me a moment," she told Mara with a nervous smile as she patted Homer and then reached into her purse to pull out her phone.

She'd been waiting for Micah to text and tell her he'd arrived at his penthouse in New York. As expected, the message was from him.

> *Micah: I'm home. Are you talking about us guys yet?*

She smiled, hating to admit he was right. The group of women *did* talk a lot about the men in their lives, but it wasn't their *only* topic of conversation. It was obvious that they were all madly in love with their guys, so the conversation about them came up naturally.

She answered.

> *Tessa: Do all men think all we talk about is them?*

> *Micah: Pretty much.*

Tessa snorted quietly, wanting to burst his bubble, but she needed to ask him a question.

> *Tessa: They're curious about my relationship with you. Mara just asked if I was banging you.*

> *Micah: Hang on a minute.*

She waited, wondering what he was doing. Maybe he hadn't actually reached his penthouse yet and was busy with other things.

Tessa startled when Mara reached out and tapped her arm. She looked up and saw that Mara was laughing, her face flushed with merriment as she turned her phone toward her.

"Read it," Mara requested.

Leaning over the table, Tessa could see that Micah had taken the moment he'd asked for to text Mara.

> Micah: Tessa isn't banging me. I'm banging her... every chance I get. Now leave the poor woman alone and let her eat. She's going to need her energy when I get back to Amesport.

Tessa was still gaping at the message on Mara's phone when hers buzzed again.

> Micah: Took care of it.

She typed a message back quickly.

> Tessa: I can't believe you just did that.

> Micah: Why? It's true.

> Tessa: But now all of your family will know.

> Micah: They know anyway. I just made it official. If you don't want to say any more, then don't.

> Tessa: I wasn't sure what to say.

> Micah: Say anything you want. We Sinclairs tend to be blunt.

Tessa: You don't care that they know?

Micah: Nope. I plan to be banging you for a very long time. Maybe I'll even let you bang me.

Tessa: I doubt it. You're too bossy.

Micah: When I get back, I'll try to let you be the boss. Okay, not much, but I'll try it once.

Tessa snickered, thinking about Micah's dominant tendencies and the probability of him letting her take control.

Tessa: Promise?

She wasn't surprised when there was a long hesitation before he answered.

Micah: I promise to try. Right now I'd do just about anything to have you naked. I miss you already.

Tessa's heart skittered and she fumbled as she typed back.

Tessa: I miss you, too. I think Homer does, too.

Before they'd left the guesthouse, the canine had come trotting into the living room with one of Micah's running shoes and dropped it at her feet, giving her a questioning look. He seemed to be asking for Micah, and the action had made her both laugh and sympathize with the dog.

Micah: Have fun and text me when you get home safe.

His fear for her safety warmed her heart.

Tessa: I hope you have a good trip.

Micah: I'll know tomorrow when I can get back.

Tessa: OK

She stuffed the phone back into her purse with a happy smile. When she looked up, she realized all of the women were watching her.

Mara turned the phone her direction again. "Spill the details," Jared's wife insisted.

Emily was sitting next to her and tapped. "We want to know. Is it serious? I didn't think Micah would ever settle down."

Then Sarah tapped. "How did you two even meet?"

Kristin tapped. "Why did he buy all that property outside of town? Is he staying?"

Tessa answered all their questions one by one, telling the women that her relationship with Micah wasn't serious, and she shared the story of how she'd originally walked into the bathroom by accident and saw him naked. She laughed and said it was lust at first sight. Then she told Kristin she wasn't entirely sure about the property, which was true. She explained that Micah didn't intend to build the property up, and that he was just building a few vacation homes for himself and his brothers.

She'd known all of the women since they were kids except Sarah— most of them were around the same age—so it was no secret to everyone except Dante's wife that Tessa had once been a figure skater, and Tessa watched as Kristin quickly and briefly explained the situation to Sarah as she told the rest of the women about why she and Micah had spent so much time together. Everyone was incredibly supportive when she told them that Micah was helping her prepare for an Olympic skating reunion.

"That's fantastic! Why didn't you tell me?" Mara asked, her fist pumping the air in excitement. "I want to go."

Emily nodded enthusiastically. "Me, too."

"And me," Kristin joined in.

"We can catch a ride with Mara and Jared," Sarah added after she tapped Tessa on the arm to let her know she wanted to join the group.

Tessa's heart clenched with emotion. "You'd all fly to New York just to see me skate? I'm not as good as I was ten years ago," she warned them.

"Of course we want to go. And you're still going to be amazing. You don't forget those kinds of skills," Mara explained.

"That's what Micah said. He's the one who talked me into skating again. He was right. I did want to skate, but I was afraid to try." She paused before adding, "Thank you. I'm touched that you all want to go. Really." Her voice cracked, and Tessa felt overwhelmed by the support she got from every woman sitting at the table.

She was casual friends with Emily, Mara, and Kristin. She'd met Sarah, but she didn't really know her. She'd never really reached out to any of them, afraid to try to befriend them because she felt so much different from these women. In reality, she wasn't different at all, and her imagined problem with communication had been just that: fear that they wouldn't accept her and that she wouldn't be able to really fit into their world.

"Why wouldn't we want to go?" Mara said, looking at Tessa questioningly. "You're our hometown Olympic champion and our friend. This is a pretty big deal for you."

Tessa looked around the table at the four women.

It was never them. It was me.

Tessa had been afraid to reach out to any of them because she'd been terrified that they'd brand her as different, avoid her because she had changed. She lived in a world without sound; they didn't. The truth was that it didn't seem to matter to them that she was deaf. The only person who had considered it was *her*. These women had always been willing to be her friends. Tessa had been the one to distance herself.

She'd stayed close to Randi because her friend had just barged back into her life without an invitation. The rest of them had allowed her to keep a comfortable distance after Tessa had lost her hearing, because it was probably what they thought she wanted. She'd always been invited to go places with them, encouraged to join them for lunches. It was *she* who had rejected *them*.

Even now, every one of them was willing to still support her, still considered her a friend. "Thank you," she said to Mara, then looked around the table. "Thank you all for wanting to be there."

Sarah tapped her arm. "We *are* going to be there. I'm sorry I never recognized you. I was never allowed to watch much television as a child, and certainly not any kind of sports. Then I was busy with medical school and my residency. If I'd been a normal person I probably would have known."

Tessa answered, "Most people don't recognize me. I used my full name of Theresa when I was skating, so people don't really even connect the name." She sensed that there was a story behind Sarah's claim that she wasn't normal, but all she knew about Dante's wife was that she was a good doctor, and had a way-higher-than-normal IQ. Maybe Sarah had been treated differently, maybe she'd felt out of place, too.

Sarah caught her attention as she questioned, "Have you ever tried cochlear implants? Kristin said you got meningitis and didn't get treatment quickly enough to stop the hearing loss. It's not my area of specialty, but I'd think you'd at least be a possible candidate."

Tessa nodded, the failed implant not as uncomfortable to talk about as it used to be. "I had one, but I got an infection and it had to be removed."

"That happens sometimes, but it's very rare. You could try again," Sarah told her, squeezing her forearm in support.

Tessa saw the kindness in Sarah's remarkable violet eyes as the two women locked gazes across the table. "Scary thought," Tessa answered simply.

"I understand. Especially after everything that's happened to you. But the odds of it occurring again are pretty low. It might be worth the risk if that's what you really want."

"I do want it," she shared with Sarah frankly. "It's only fear that's held me back." She wasn't going to try to use the excuse of expense, because the money it would cost wasn't the real reason she wasn't trying to get the implant again. Pure and simple—she had been terrified of another loss or failure.

"Understandable," Sarah replied. "I think I'd be afraid to ever try again, too."

All the women nodded emphatically around the table, agreeing with Sarah's statement wholeheartedly. The solidarity and support of her emotions made Tessa want to cry.

How long had she needed validation?

How long had she needed to hear that she wasn't wrong?

How long had she needed to pull her friends closer instead of keeping them at a distance?

How long had she felt alone and isolated?

Too. Damn. Long.

Tessa took a deep breath and asked, "I want to look into it, Sarah. Can you help me? I'm not sure what the medical protocol is if I've already had one implant that had to be removed."

Sarah smiled at her. "Of course. It isn't your fault it failed, so I wouldn't think it would be an issue for your insurance company, but I'll check everything out. I have a colleague in New York who is considered one of the best in the country with this procedure. I can contact her. Maybe you can see her while you're in New York City?"

Tessa nodded jerkily. "Yes, please. I'd like that. I had it done in Boston last time. I think maybe having it done somewhere else would help. I don't exactly have great memories of Boston. I'd rather not go there." Not only had she lost her hearing in Boston, but she had too many bad memories of Rick to be happy about going back there. This would be a new beginning for her. She wanted to start it in a new place.

"I'd be happy to set it up," Sarah told her with a smile.

Mara tapped Tessa's arm. "Now that we have the medical stuff taken care of, let's hear more about you and Micah. Are my cousins going to start moving to Amesport permanently? I'd love that."

Tessa laughed. "Don't get your hopes up. You know how Micah rolls. He always needs the next adrenaline rush. But I think he's pretty happy in New York. He loves his company, and his passion is making extreme sports safer."

Emily tapped her arm. "Does that scare you? The crazy stuff he does?"

Tessa thought for a minute before replying. "I care about him now, and I won't say that I wouldn't worry about him if he was doing something dangerous. But his passions are part of who Micah is, and he's a good man. I wouldn't want to change him. Besides, I went skydiving with him, and I loved it."

She looked at the shocked expressions around the table and added, "What? You think a deaf woman can't skydive?" Tessa was determined that she'd get her certification to go solo someday, even though Micah didn't seem too keen to have her jump out of a plane unless she was attached to him.

All of the other women were shaking their heads, as though most of them wouldn't even think about jumping out of a perfectly good plane.

Funny, she'd thought the same thing until she'd met Micah. Maybe she'd had a dream that someday she'd be brave enough to try, but everybody had dreams that would never be fulfilled. When it came right down to it, Tessa wasn't sure if she would have really jumped with anybody except Micah. But after that experience, she could totally understand why he loved the adrenaline rush.

Their food arrived and all of them dug into their plates enthusiastically. Tessa slipped Homer a few pieces of chicken from her lo mein noodle dish, even though she knew she shouldn't. He rewarded her with a worshipful doggie expression that made her chuckle.

The women managed to keep chattering while they ate, and the evening was over so soon that Tessa couldn't believe that it was already ten o'clock when they left the restaurant. They all hugged like they didn't reside in the same small town, and Tessa relished every minute of it. Physical contact was her bond with other people, and it felt good to feel this close to these women.

After everyone made sure that Tessa had their numbers in her phone, she beckoned Homer to jump into her little economy car. He took up the entire passenger's seat, and he was watchful as she walked around the vehicle and got into the driver's side.

"I'll bet all that girl talk wasn't much fun for you, was it, boy?" she said to Homer as she stroked his silky head. "Let's go home. I'll find you a real treat."

The canine leaned over and licked her cheek before settling into his seat.

Tessa laughed as she started the car, thinking how pivotal the night had been for her. Not only had she bonded with four women she admired, but her dog seemed content just to be with her, too.

Her life had begun to change so much, so many of her fears so much easier to face because she realized that much of her anxiety was self-inflicted. They were her insecurities, her self-doubt.

"I'm done with all that," she shared with Homer as she pulled out of her parking spot and headed back to Randi's old home.

Years ago, she'd sworn that she was going to find herself again. Now she felt like maybe, just possibly, she was going to figure out exactly who she was for the very first time.

She drove home content with her epiphany, because she was pretty sure she was going to like the person she dug out from underneath her frightened, deaf exterior. Hopefully, she'd like that woman very much.

CHAPTER 17

Having a canine companion brought more joy into Tessa's life than she ever could have imagined. She went for a run with her dog the next morning, and he actually kept pace alongside of her as she jogged at a steady speed. She slowed occasionally, worried that poor Homer might be exhausted, but the dog was full of energy. He spurred her on when she would have given him a rest.

When they were at the rink, her dog clambered up a few rows in the old stands so he could see her, watching her silently, his gaze always alert.

Tessa hadn't bothered with the music because Micah wasn't around to give her signals, but she skated her entire routine, including the extended position hold at the very end.

That was when she saw a man standing directly in front of her clapping his hands, applauding her performance. She moved closer to see who had been watching her, suddenly feeling apprehensive. It wasn't Micah. She didn't expect him back until tomorrow. She stopped at the wall, the only thing separating the two of them, when she realized who exactly she was seeing, although she still couldn't quite believe it.

Rick? What the hell is he doing in Amesport, Maine?

She stared, noticing that even though he was only a year or two older than Micah, he looked older than that. He'd put on weight. Not that she'd say he was fat, but he'd definitely indulged in too much rich food and too much alcohol during the years they'd been apart.

Her eyes went automatically to his mouth when it started to move.

"I have to say, that was extraordinary, Tessa. You got your hearing back? I saw that you were on the performance schedule for New York. You skate as gracefully as you did years ago."

Her mind whirling just from the impact of seeing her first love after so long, Tessa could barely find the words to say. This man had devastated her, but her heart didn't seem to care. After a moment of surprise . . . she felt . . . nothing. No, maybe that wasn't true. She felt angry.

"What do you want, Rick?" she asked flatly.

"I saw that you were skating again, and I just decided I needed to make the trip to see you. You've matured nicely, Tessa. I've missed you."

She watched as Homer climbed down from the stands, his gaze pensive as he sat some distance away from Rick, as though he didn't trust him.

Don't worry, Homer. I don't trust him, either.

"You decided you had to see me after all these years? Why?" She felt her body tense.

"We had something together, Tessa. Maybe we gave it up too easily. I haven't been able to find anyone like you again."

Rage boiled inside her, a fury that she hadn't realized still existed. "Oh, you mean after you kicked me out of your home and moved another woman in? Or after you dumped me at one of the lowest points of my life."

"I loved you, Tessa. I just didn't know how to deal with your handicap. But now that you can hear again—"

"No!" she shouted at him. For an instant, she was thrown back to the life they'd had together. It had been good, but only when she was his perfectly behaved, champion figure skater who was molded to be exactly as he wanted her. "*I* learned to deal with being deaf, and I am not handicapped. And I don't need you anymore. I don't think I ever did."

"You're right. You're not handicapped *now*," Rick pointed out. "Come back to me, Tessa. Things can be like they were before. We put a lot of years and a lot of work into our relationship. You can't just forget that. I even still have your ring." He pulled a small box out of his pocket and popped it open.

It was the diamond she'd worn on her finger, the very ring whose loss had made her finger feel bare and empty for quite some time after their breakup.

He must be between women if he came searching me out. Or no other woman but a naive eighteen-year-old would put up with him. What the hell? Does he think I'm still the trainable girl I used to be?

Tessa shuddered. The last thing she could imagine was going back to the way she was before. In this one area, her hearing loss had probably been a blessing. It had taught her what love *wasn't*, and she hadn't ended up married to the most selfish man on Earth.

"Funny, I seem to remember that you said we fell out of love," she reminded him, portions of that last conversation with him floating through her brain, a discussion that had once hurt her so much.

"I know what I said, but I'm ready to take you back now." His expression turned dark and irritated.

Tessa skated down to the wall opening, and Homer came to greet her. She patted the dog on the head and then took her skates off quickly, slipping on her shoes. Then, she stuffed the skates into the bag she'd brought with her and put the straps over her shoulder, ignoring Rick completely until she had to pass him on the way out.

He gripped her arm, keeping her from leaving. "Did you hear me? I said I'm ready to take you back."

She had to hold back a laugh as she looked at his annoyed expression. Did he really think she'd go crawling back to him that easily? For what? Money? Honestly, he really was a dick. How had she never seen that before? How had she ever been with a man like him?

I was young and easily led because I knew nothing about relationships. My whole life revolved around skating. Then it also revolved around him.

She'd put just as much effort into pleasing Rick as she had the figure-skating judges, and she really had lost everything she was or could have been in the process. She *had* lost herself, any identity that she would have developed from her own ideas, her own experiences. Because she'd loved skating, she hadn't minded trying to please the judges. With Rick, she'd had a choice, but she'd been convinced that she loved him, and she forgave herself for being a fool. Unfortunately, he didn't seem to understand that she was all grown up now.

She shrugged out of his hold, and when he went to grab her arm again, Homer bared his teeth. By the frightened look on Rick's face, she assumed her canine was giving him a warning growl.

She patted her thigh, and Homer came up beside her, walking at her side as she truly left her past behind. Her relationship with Micah might be finite, destined to end in the near future, but she realized she'd rather spend five minutes with Micah Sinclair than a lifetime of hell with somebody who didn't give a damn about her.

Rick followed and came stomping out the door as she held it open for him, then shut it behind him to lock it.

His expression was outraged as she looked at him in the sunlight. "You're making a big mistake, Tessa. Women would kill to be my wife."

"I might *kill you* if I was your wife," she shot back. "You're a controlling, pretentious bastard who treats women like they're garbage. I'm not the same woman I was back then, thank God." She waved him off. She was done. "Go find yourself a woman who values the same things you do. I don't."

She started walking toward her car with Homer before she called over her shoulder, "By the way, I'm still deaf, but I'm definitely not handicapped. I've just realized that I can still skate with or without my hearing. Now go back to Boston. There's nothing here in Maine for you."

He'd have much better luck in a bigger city finding another gullible girl. Tessa was already pitying any woman who hooked up with him.

She never looked back as she drove away, but she did smile as Homer licked her face and then settled into his seat.

She got a text later in the day from Julian, letting her know that he was due to land shortly with Xander in tow. He asked if she could possibly go to Evan's guesthouse to make sure there was no alcohol or pills in the residence.

Tessa took Homer with her, and, as she poured out the last bottle of beer, she wondered what would become of Micah's brother.

She sighed as she took the trash out and dumped it, knowing the guest residence was now empty of any type of substance that could send Xander off the wagon.

Granted, her heart ached for Micah's youngest brother. He'd been there for her at a time in her life when she'd really needed a friendly face. Back then, he'd been the type of man to reach out to a complete stranger and make sure she was safe. Did he realize that he was now ripping his family apart?

What kind of guy was he now?

She'd vacuumed and dusted the guesthouse, cleaning up as well as she could on short notice. With little else to do, she put on a pot of coffee.

Seconds later, Homer came bouncing into the kitchen to signal her, and she followed him to the front door.

"Somebody is here?" she asked the dog needlessly since he'd already identified the door as the place where he was hearing noise.

Flipping the deadbolt, she gripped the handle and pulled, seeing two men standing at the top step. Moving back as she recognized Julian, she tried not to stare at the guy he currently had by the collar of his black leather jacket. Julian steered Xander through the house and into the kitchen, shoving his ass down in a chair at the table.

"I have to hit the shower," Julian announced angrily. "The little bastard sprayed me with a can of Coke I offered him when he said he wanted a drink."

Julian stomped toward the bathroom with an overnight bag slung over his shoulder.

She turned her back and busied herself with making two cups of coffee, placing cream and sugar on the table because she had no idea what either man put in their coffee. For that matter, she didn't even know if they *liked* coffee.

If she didn't know that this was the same Xander she'd come to like during a single rescue and a car ride, she never would have recognized him. He had a scraggly beard that could use trimming, longer hair, and, although she'd only gotten a brief glance at his face, he was scarred. He was also thin, too thin.

Putting one mug in front of him with a spoon, she took the other cup and sat across from him, adding cream to her coffee before she spoke. "How are you, Xander? Do you remember me?"

His hand moved slightly to wrap around the coffee mug.

"Please don't throw it at me. The coffee is hot," she reminded him.

Tessa noticed his hands were shaking slightly, and his eyes looked lifeless as he stared at the mug, probably trying to decide whether or not to vent his anger by tossing it.

"If you don't like coffee, I'll get you something else," she offered.

"I. Want. A. Damn. Drink."

Had he not enunciated, Tessa might have had a difficult time understanding what he said because of his facial hair. "You have a drink. There isn't a drop of alcohol anywhere in the house. There's soda, which you've obviously rudely refused. Or that coffee in front of you."

"You're the deaf chick I met years ago."

She nodded. "Yes."

"You still can't hear?"

Tessa shook her head. "No."

"Good." He took the mug and pitched it, slamming it against the refrigerator and causing it to shatter. "Glad you didn't hear that."

Tessa gave a cry of dismay as she saw the coffee pooled on the floor with the glass, the dark liquid scattered all over the cupboards and the fridge.

She stood and put her hands on her hips. "What exactly was the point of that?"

"Unless you can get me a real drink or get me laid, you can just leave me the fuck alone. There's only two things I want right now. Coffee isn't one of them."

Tessa crouched and started collecting the glass on the tile. "What in the hell is wrong with you?"

"I'm a dick," he said with a shrug.

"You didn't used to be." She looked up at him.

"That was a long time ago."

Xander was silent while Tessa cleaned up the mess, cutting her finger in the process as she trashed the glass.

"Dammit!" she cried as she saw the blood running down her palm from the cut.

Xander got up and took her hand lightly, cleaning the injury in the sink. It was superficial and stopped bleeding almost instantly. He directed her back to her chair and pushed on her shoulders, forcing her to sit.

She watched as he finished mopping up the mess before he sat down again.

Homer, who had been watching from the door of the kitchen, went to Xander, sniffed him, then promptly laid his head in his lap.

Tessa held her breath, hoping Xander hadn't changed so much that he'd rebuff or kick an innocent dog. She let out the air as she saw Micah's youngest brother put his hand on Homer's head and stroke it absently.

"You know you're hurting your brothers. Were you trying to die, or was it an accident?" Tessa figured she had nothing to lose by asking. Xander could throw another temper fit, but he was out of ready ammunition since she had her fingers through the handle of her mug, and she'd put the cream and sugar away while she was cleaning up the mess he'd made.

He ignored her question and slumped into the chair as though he'd rather be anywhere but there. "I won't stay on the wagon, if that's what they're hoping. Why can't they just leave me alone?"

"Because they love you," Tessa told him sternly. "You're their brother. Don't tell me you wouldn't do the same thing." She paused before adding, "I tried to kill myself once. It was after I came back home. My parents died, so I really did lose everything I loved."

He looked at her with a slight bit of interest. "Then why are you still alive?"

"I stopped before it was too late. I thought about my brother, my only living relative, and I didn't want to leave him alone and feeling guilty because he couldn't save me. That's what would happen if you died. Neither of your brothers would ever forgive themselves."

"I'm not trying to die, okay? I just need to escape. The alcohol and pills help."

"No, they don't. They'll ultimately be what kills you," Tessa shot back at him.

"Then maybe I do fucking want to die. Christ! I wish everybody would just leave me the hell alone. My brothers would still have each other and our cousins. They don't need me."

Xander emanated a darkness that Tessa could feel. "I can't say that I know how you feel. It had to be horrible seeing your parents die. But there will eventually be light. I promise you." Her heart squeezed as she looked at the man Xander had become.

"My brothers don't know everything, and because I'm a goddamn coward, they never will. But there is no light at the end of my long-ass tunnel. It's fucking infinite."

"And you're dragging Micah and Julian along with you," Tessa informed him. "Did you know Micah's headaches are back, probably triggered by stress? Can't you at least try?" she begged.

"I'll fail," Xander said nonchalantly. "The nightmares get me whether I'm awake or asleep, without my pills or my alcohol."

"You can get past that," Tessa told him, desperately wanting to reach the old Xander that she had liked so long ago. He was still there. He had to be.

"No, I can't." He rose. "I'm going to bed. Tell Julian I don't need a fucking babysitter."

Tessa knew Xander was going to get a nanny whether he wanted one or not. Julian was staying here with him.

"Maybe if you tried to tell them everything—"

Xander glared at her as he spoke. "I don't need to talk. I need to be stoned. So either bring me a willing woman or a drink, or shut the hell up."

She stopped talking because he walked away. He was right. If he didn't solve his underlying problems, he was going to fail rehab.

A tear slid down her cheek, wondering what had happened to Xander to make him so bitter and angry. Maybe he did just want to forget what he'd seen the night his parents were murdered, but there was more to the story. He'd admitted as much.

Homer moved over to her and put his head on her lap, and Tessa stroked his silky head as she wondered what or who could get through to Xander.

She knew it wasn't her.

Unfortunately, she'd just failed miserably.

CHAPTER 18

"He's going to break your heart. When he's ready to go, he'll leave and he won't look back," Liam told Tessa as they sat at one of the sadly worn tables at Sullivan's Steak and Seafood the next evening.

Tessa had filled in for one of their waitresses who'd needed the night off. Micah had texted that he'd be home the next morning, and she couldn't wait to see him.

Honestly, she knew that her brother was right. She *would* pay for indulging herself in Micah's passion. But even now, she wouldn't trade the experience to avoid the inevitable pain. "It will be my issue to deal with," she told her brother sternly.

Liam shrugged as he took a gulp of the beer in front of him. "I don't want to see you hurt."

Her heart squeezed forcefully in her chest as she looked at her forlorn sibling. "You can't protect me from everything, Liam. I'm almost twenty-eight years old. I like Micah, and he's the first guy I've wanted to spend time with since Rick."

"He's the first guy who ever got the chance," Liam argued.

Tessa shook her head. "He's the only one I wanted." Desperate to change the subject, she told him, "I finally looked in my bank account.

Liam, there has to be a mistake. Where did all that money come from? Is it yours?"

"No. The money is yours. Tessa, Mom and Dad were far from being poor. And they got the restaurant and money from Grandma and Grandpa when they passed away. Plus, we make a good profit here. That's your half of your inheritance and the profit from the restaurant. Once I sell the house, you'll get half of that, too."

"But there's almost a million dollars in my account. That can't possibly be right. I almost had a heart attack when I looked earlier today."

Liam lifted his eyebrow. "You just noticed? Tessa, we've had the joint account with the inheritance and profits for years. How in the hell did you not notice?"

"I didn't look. I didn't want to look."

"Why the hell not?"

"I don't know." She sighed. "Never mind. I *do* know. I think I was making excuses not to try to have the implants again. I wanted you to take the inheritance from Mom and Dad. I didn't care how much it was. Neither of them talked much about money. I wanted to believe we didn't have the funds, and whatever we had needed to go toward refurbishing the restaurant."

"I already have a fund set up for that, Tessa. I've been saving from our profits. I got an estimate over the summer. It's covered. I just need a slow period where we can get the work done." He hesitated before he questioned, "Do you *want* to try again? You've been pretty adamant about not doing it. I thought you didn't want to take the risk. To tell you the truth, I don't know if I would, either, if I had been through all of the shit you have in the last six years."

"I think I might," she ventured hesitantly. "Sarah has a doctor friend in New York who's one of the best in the country with the procedure. I'd like to at least see her when I'm in the city. What happened to me was rare. I can't blow off the chance to at least find out all of the facts."

Liam rose quickly to his feet and scooped her up and swung her around. As he set her on her feet again, he looked excited. "That's my brave sister. I think it would be fantastic if you tried."

She hugged him back. "I was scared, Liam. I've been scared for a long time of so many things."

He took her by the shoulders. "And you're not anymore?"

"I wouldn't say that," she answered drily. "But I won't let my fears rule my life anymore. If I don't try it, I'll never know if I could have had my hearing back again."

"You are brave, Tessa. Hell, you're one of the gutsiest women I know. I may not be too sure about your choice in men, but you've always handled things better than I would have done."

She put a hand on his shoulder, Liam's support and the way he'd always been beside her bringing tears to her eyes. She wasn't about to tell him about the times when she was weak, when her world was pitch-dark. He didn't need to know, and she was over her past. Tessa wanted to move forward, and she wanted Liam to do the same.

She smiled through her tears. "You're the best brother a woman could ever ask for. Everything I've gone through, you've suffered right along with me. It's time for us to be happy, Liam, and it's time to let go of any notion that you're responsible for any of the tragedies that happened in the past."

"But what if—"

She quickly covered his mouth with her hand. "No more what-ifs for either of us. Please. Our life is good. And I've suddenly become a millionaire." She giggled as she removed her hand from his mouth. "Looking at my savings was like winning the lottery."

"Did you really think you had to work those other jobs?"

She shrugged. "I guess I did, but only because I chose to believe it. Besides, I get bored when you won't let me work here more."

"Somebody would lose their job," he warned her.

"I know. That's why I find other things to do. Even now that I know I'm loaded, I'll still do those jobs. But I'm not moving back home," she warned him. "I'm too old to live with my brother. It's not much different from still living with parents. I'm independent and able to function just fine on my own."

She could buy her own place now, own property. The shock of finding out that she actually had a lot of money still had her head spinning.

"You're always going to be my little sister," Liam said, tugging her ponytail playfully.

Tessa laughed, knowing she could handle Liam being the protective older brother. What she couldn't deal with was his guilt and over-the-top need to keep her safe.

"So I guess this means my brother is even a better catch than I thought," Tessa said thoughtfully.

Liam frowned. "Don't even try to set me up again."

"But you have as much money as me, right?"

He smirked at her. "More. I told you that I developed some products early in my career. I sold some of them and I collect some fat and happy royalties. I also get paid very well for consulting. I am the best in my field."

"So you're rich?" Tessa asked bluntly as she gaped at her brother.

"Not *Sinclair* type of rich, but yeah, I'm not hurting for cash. Jesus, why didn't you ask me before?" he asked, clearly frustrated.

"I don't think I was ready to face reality," she admitted. "I guess I was content just to work when I could and convince myself that I was okay the way I was."

"You *are* okay," Liam answered quickly. "More than okay."

"No, I wasn't. I was scared, but I was safe in my small little world where I couldn't do much." Where there were boundaries, there was security.

"So you aren't going to be brokenhearted when you're staring at the backside of Sinclair?"

She thought for a minute. "I *will* be sad. Maybe I'll even fall apart for a while. But I wouldn't trade meeting Micah for any reason. He's the reason I'm skating, he's the reason I'm trying. He's the reason I want so much more than I've had before."

"You're in love with him," Liam stated flatly.

She nodded as tears began to flood her cheeks.

Liam put his arms around her and pulled his little sister tightly against him, then kissed her on the top of her head. "If he hurts you, I'll kill him."

Tessa didn't hear him; she just continued to cry.

Later that night, she awoke to Homer rolling against her body as the mattress beneath her compressed.

Tessa sprang out of bed and flipped on the bedside lamp. Her heart continued to race in surprise, but she couldn't help but laugh.

Micah was sprawled on the bed facedown, Homer sitting next to him looking affronted and unhappy.

Tessa took her time admiring Micah's nude body, his tight ass and ripped biceps flexing as he slowly rose on his hands and knees and flopped with his back against the headboard.

Man and dog glared at each other before Micah finally asked, "You let the dog sleep on my side of the bed?"

"Well, you weren't here," she answered logically. "And he likes the bed."

"I like it, too," Micah answered, looking disgruntled.

She bit her lip to keep from laughing before asking, "Why *are* you here? I thought you were coming in the morning."

He grinned at her. "I decided I needed to *come* now. I missed you. I knew I wasn't going to sleep, so I decided to just fly back."

Her body melted, and liquid heat flooded between her thighs. Micah was sitting on her bed, looking tired but gorgeous, and she wanted to touch him . . . right now.

She patted her bare thigh, and Homer immediately left the bed and jumped to the floor. Absently, she stroked his silky head, realizing she was wearing very little clothing herself. The nightshirt she wore ended at the tops of her thighs, and the matching panties didn't exactly qualify as underwear. They were more like a thong, barely covering her pussy and leaving her ass bare.

Clambering back into the bed, Tessa put her arms around Micah's neck, and his arms immediately wrapped around her. She laid her head on his chest, warmth flooding her soul as they stayed in that embrace, simply enjoying the feel of each other.

"Jesus, I'm glad I came back," Micah told her as he pulled her head back so she could see him. "If I had to wait until tomorrow, I don't think I would have been worth a shit."

Her heart skipped a beat and then accelerated as she saw the covetous look in his eyes. "I missed you, too. How was your inspection?"

"There were a couple of minor issues or I would have been back yesterday. But I'm done."

She licked her lips, her mouth suddenly dry. God, he was warm and inviting. Her body craved him, while her mind knew they needed sleep. "I'm sure you're tired."

"Not *that* tired," he denied. "I was pissed off because all I wanted was to be with you."

"I probably got more sleep than you, so move down and let me do the work." He'd promised to give her control, and she planned on taking him up on that offer. "You did promise."

"Baby, all I want is to be inside you as quickly as possible right now." His face was dark with need.

"I'll get you there." Tessa wanted the same thing, craved it.

He moved down so his head hit the pillow, never taking his eyes from her. "Now," he demanded, running a hand down her belly and stroking her saturated pussy through the skimpy panties. "You're already wet for me, sweet Tessa?"

She was beyond wet; she was desperate. "Yes."

Anxious to feel his body skin-to-skin, she pulled the cotton nightshirt over her head and tossed it to the floor.

Homer moved as the nightie landed near his body. The canine promptly got up and scampered out of the bedroom, finding a safer place to lie in the living room.

Micah ran a frustrated hand through his hair as Tessa shimmied out of her barely-there panties. "I need this. I need you so damn much that I can't think straight."

The smoldering heat in his eyes caused her core to clench almost painfully as she straddled him, her moist heat connecting with his muscular abs.

"Oh, God. Me, too," she confessed. "I'm glad you're here."

How did she explain that when he was there, she felt ravenous, her body and soul longing to crawl inside him and never come out?

Micah got to her like no other man ever had.

Unable to stop herself, she lowered her head and kissed him.

CHAPTER 19

Micah was doubtful that he was going to last very long. Hell, Tessa had haunted his dreams day and night. When he wasn't fucking dreaming about being inside her, he was thinking about it.

Yeah, he'd worried about her while he was in New York, but more than that, he just wanted to *see* her again, *touch* her again.

He took little comfort in the fact that she had a new dog for company. *He* wanted to be at her side. *He* wanted to be with her. Shit, he was almost jealous of a damn dog that had shared her bed while he was gone!

He fisted her hair, pulling her mouth harder against his. The intimacy was satisfying, but after the torment of missing her for the last few days, it wasn't enough. He could feel her liquid heat against his stomach, and he wanted to be inside her with an obsession he couldn't control.

Pulling her hair just hard enough to break the embrace, he forewarned her, "If I'm not inside you in the next three seconds, I'm going to do it myself."

Why in the hell did I promise to let her take control? Granted, she looks hot as hell on top of me, grinding her hips against me, her curly hair fanning out from her beautiful face with an expression so needy that it's tearing me apart.

Taking a hand from her hair, he said demandingly, "One!" He held up one finger.

"You promised," she said as she sat up and slid down his body slowly, leaving a trail of liquid heat on his lower abdomen.

His other hand fell from her silky locks and he immediately cupped one of her ample breasts, gritting his teeth as he noticed that her nipple was already peaked and hard.

"Two!" He held up another finger, letting it join the first.

"Wait! I'm not used to this. I've never done it before," she said anxiously.

Jesus! She's never ridden a guy to oblivion before?

Micah realized that he'd never given her a chance. He was always desperate for her, and he immediately took the lead, never giving her an opportunity to ride him. Obviously, her ex hadn't let her have her way with him, either.

He tried to clear his mind of any other man touching Tessa. It made him too crazy.

The muscles in his jaw tightened as Tessa fumbled with his rock-hard cock.

"Two and a half!" He didn't add another finger to the count.

Tessa looked flustered, and he knew he was going to have to wait, but the tutoring would be worth it.

He took both his hands and grasped her hips. "Guide me in, slowly lower yourself down," he rasped desperately, pushing her hips down as he flexed his groin upward.

A powerful groan left his mouth as he felt her muscles tightening around him. He went deeper . . . and then deeper still.

"Three!" he said with immense relief and intense satisfaction as her slick muscles engulfed him completely, and he was buried inside her to the root of his dick, exactly where he needed to be.

He was already damp with sweat, his control on a hair trigger. "Ride me, baby," he commanded. "Now!"

"How?" she asked uncertainly as she ground down with her hips experimentally. "God, you feel so deep like this."

Micah fucking loved that, going deep, and he did feel completely consumed. "Any way you want to. Just move."

He was starting to sweat bullets as he ached for release. But he wasn't coming before she did. Ladies always came first.

"Are you my horse?" she asked with a sultry smile. "I'm starting to feel like a cowgirl."

"I'm whatever the hell you want me to be," he confessed hoarsely as he held her hips tightly and withdrew, then thrust back up.

"Oh," she murmured, her head falling back as a sexy moan escaped from her mouth.

"I've never ridden a horse," she admitted as she panted, her hands moving to her breasts, tweaking her nipples as she lifted her hips and slammed back down onto his cock.

"Yeah, sweetheart. Take your pleasure," Micah encouraged, even though he knew she couldn't see his words. He was caught up in the moment, watching the sensual creature on top of him with a combination of awe and carnal lust.

She moved gracefully, her body catching the motion of his upward thrusts, meeting his over and over until she fell into a furious rhythm that was driving him to the point of madness. His balls tightened, his body clamoring for release, but he held back as much as he could, watching completely enthralled as Tessa's hands pleasured her breasts, moaning with every collision of their groins, looking lost in her own desires.

"So good, Micah. It feels so good." Her head fell forward again, her long curls covering her face as she finally stopped torturing her nipples and rested her hands on his shoulders. "I need to come so bad."

Micah's heart and hand responded to her desire. Without stopped his punishing strokes upward, he pressed a hand between their bodies and found her clit, stroking over the slick nub with the force he knew she wanted right now.

"Oh, God. Yes. Please," she whimpered.

He felt her body begin to tighten, her muscles starting to wrap around his cock like a well-fitting glove.

He swiped the hair from her face, flipping it carelessly backward so he could see her.

Her expression was the mixture of agony and ecstasy that was always present when she was on the verge of climax, and her scream of pleasure was his undoing.

"Micah!"

The sound of his name on her lips as she crested sent him over the edge. He thrust up hard, letting her milk him of his own orgasm, and he groaned helplessly as his hands went to her ass. He gripped it hard as he exploded inside her with a force that rocked his entire world.

She collapsed on top of him, completely spent, and he savored the contact of their damp bodies skin-to-skin. He stroked her hair as she panted and laid her head on his still-heaving chest.

Mine! This woman is my other half, the part of me that's always been missing.

Maybe he'd thought Beatrice was more than a little bit crazy, but of all the women in the world, she *had* figured out the one who fit him just right, found the woman who would make him whole.

It just so happened that Micah had that very woman sprawled across his body right now, and there was no place he'd rather be than beneath her, cradling her body against his. His mind, soul, and body were completely at peace.

Tessa stirred and started to separate them. "I'm heavy," she murmured.

He turned her face to his as he said, "Stay and kiss me."

She frowned at him, but she didn't move. "Still bossy? I thought I was the boss right now."

Tessa had no idea that *she* was his Achilles' heel, his greatest weakness, yet still his greatest source of strength. It was an uncomfortable position to be in, but he was getting used to it. Hell, he'd give her anything she wanted if she'd just fucking kiss him. "Do it," he said huskily.

She smiled at him as she lowered her head a little. "Okay. But only because I want to."

Micah closed his eyes as he felt the warmth of her breath on his lips, and his heart began to pound against the wall of his chest as she gave him the sweetest kiss he'd ever had.

"Okay?" she asked as she pulled back.

"Yeah." He nodded, pulling her back against him.

What am I going to do with her? What's going to happen if I can't convince her that we can make this work forever?

He listened to her breathing slow as she fell asleep, his eyes closing as his arms tightened around her body protectively.

As he drifted into sleep, Micah realized there were no "ifs" for him, no pondering failure. He needed Tessa like he needed his next breath. Failure wasn't an option.

For the first time in his life, he'd found the woman he couldn't live without, and he had no intention of letting her go.

Micah fell into a dreamless sleep, not even stirring when Homer came back into the room, hopped up on the bed, and took an available space next to the two of them with a happy doggie sigh.

⌒

"I found out I'm rich," Tessa told Micah excitedly the next morning as they sat at the breakfast table.

Micah looked up from his food, surprised. "What? I thought you just said you're rich."

She smiled at him. "Okay, I'm not rich like you are, but I have money."

He listened closely as Tessa told him how much money she'd discovered in her bank account, and about her talk with Liam the day before.

"I've decided to try the implants again, Micah," she told him softly. "I know for sure I have the funds now, I'm dealing with reality, and I have no reason not to try."

He'd been planning on paying anything she needed to pay to get the implants if that's what she really wanted, and it rankled just a little that he doubted that she'd let him. Now that she knew she had funds, she wasn't the type of woman to take advantage of the offer he'd planned on making.

"When?" he asked cautiously.

"Sarah has a doctor friend in New York. She set me up to see her while I'm there. I'm going to have a consult to see if it's even advisable for me to try again."

"I don't see why not. If you were a candidate before, then I would think you still are." He was happy that Tessa had found the strength to try again, but now *he* was nervous.

With all of her disappointments in the past, and so many tragic events behind her, the last thing he wanted was for her to ever hurt or be sad again. He consoled himself with the fact that he'd be there for her now and in the future if pain found its way back into her life. He knew Tessa, and Micah realized that she needed to try.

"I'm nervous, but I'll be okay with whatever happens. I think the not knowing would be worse than knowing that it doesn't work," Tessa explained.

Micah knew he'd feel the same way, but her courage—still present even after so many bad things had happened to her—still humbled him sometimes.

He took her hand. "It will work, Tessa."

She squeezed his hand. "Even if it doesn't, I'll be okay."

"I'll go with you." It wasn't really an offer; it was fact. He *was* going to be there with her.

"It's after the performance. I thought maybe you'd be going back to work," she said hesitantly.

"I've been working," he growled. "Even though I'm here, I'm still working remotely. I can go with you."

She finally nodded. "I'd like that, since I assumed you wouldn't be coming back to Amesport."

"Who said I'm not coming back?" he rasped. "I'm trying to get as much of the builds up as possible before the snow starts flying, and Julian and I need to deal with Xander. There's a rehab with great results in Massachusetts. I'm hoping we can convince him to go before we leave for New York. But if I can't, I'm not sure where we'll go from there."

Shit! His fucking heart was bleeding, and Tessa was *already* writing him off?

"Julian said he was handling Xander, and I guessed since you had so many men working on the houses, you'd just leave somebody in charge," Tessa said quietly.

Honestly, he could easily do that, but then he'd have to be away from Tessa, and good-bye wasn't a word he was planning to say to her. Ever. He just hadn't told her that yet.

He pulled his hand back, wondering if she *wanted* him to stay in New York. "I guess I haven't exactly planned what was going to happen."

"Micah, don't feel like you have to stay because of me, because you're worried about hurting me. You did a lot for me, made me step out of my comfort zone and succeed. I knew what I was getting into when all this started. I knew it wasn't forever. I can handle things alone. I've done it before. I don't need you to be here."

He glared at her, seeing the regret on her face. Holy hell, *she* was blowing *him* off? It was ironic that at one time he'd worried about hurting her when he had to return to New York. "What about the performance?"

She wrung her hands together nervously, ignoring the food on her plate. "I'll need you there, but if you want to teach somebody else to do it—"

"I'm doing it," he said evenly as he stood up, unable to sit here knowing she wanted him gone.

"Thank you," she answered in a tremulous voice as she stood.

He put up a hand. "It's not a big deal. I was planning on attending anyway. It is my charity."

Micah attempted to bury his pain. If Tessa didn't feel the same way he did, he didn't know what else to say right now. She didn't need him around. For him, the rules had changed. For her, they obviously hadn't.

He needed to get away, and he needed to do it quickly. "I have to go."

"You don't want to run this morning? Or practice?"

He shook his head. "Like you said, I have a lot to do. And you don't need me anymore." He motioned toward the couch. "I picked you up a few things while I was in New York. I thought you might need them."

He didn't wait to see what she said. Saying two words he thought he'd never say, he muttered, "Good-bye, Tessa."

Swiping up his keys from the table, he turned his back on her and walked away, exiting through the front door and striding to his truck.

He knew if he turned around, he'd make a complete ass out of himself, so he got in his truck and never looked back.

CHAPTER 20

A week later, Tessa wasn't any less depressed than she'd been the moment Micah had walked out the door.

"Seriously? You just told him you didn't need him anymore?" Randi said, signing with her words as they sat in the living room of Evan and Randi's home.

She was glad to have her friend back, but Randi had been digging for information since the day she and Evan had returned a few days ago.

"I didn't blow him off, Randi, I *had* to let go. I knew Micah wasn't going to stay forever, and I was starting to feel like he was only coming back for me. I was getting too attached; things were getting too intense. I was afraid if I didn't let him know that I would be okay without him, I'd beg him to stay forever. I can't do that to him. He did so much for me."

By now, Randi knew the whole story, everything that had happened since the day Micah showed up with her naked in the shower.

Randi gave her a doubtful look. "And *are* you okay?"

Tessa's eyes welled up with tears, something that had been happening since the day Micah left Amesport to return to New York, which was just a few days after Micah had told her good-bye.

After a meeting with all of the family in town present, Xander had reluctantly agreed to go to the rehab facility, and Micah and Julian had gone with him to make sure he got settled before leaving to return to their primary homes. Tessa wondered how long Xander's rehab would last. More than likely, Xander had crushed under family pressure, but at least he'd taken the first step.

"No," she admitted. "I'm not okay. I feel like my heart is so shattered that I'll never be able to put it back together again. How stupid was I to think I could just have a fling with someone like Micah? How stupid was I to think I wouldn't be completely devastated when he finally left? I knew I was going to hurt, but it's even worse than I imagined."

"And how dumb was he to think he could just screw a woman like you?" Randi shot back. "Evan saw him in New York today. If it makes you feel any better, he's not handling this very well, either. Evan said he looks like hell, and was drowning his sorrows in a bottle of Scotch. Doesn't sound like either one of you was prepared for what happened."

"Evan saw Micah?" Tessa asked breathlessly.

Randi nodded. "He's in New York overnight. I decided to stay home because I have a lot to do for the planning on the new school. Sometimes I think I should have just gone with Evan. I think we text every half hour or so. You'd think we'd be sick of each other after our long vacation together. We were almost never apart."

"I think that's how it is when you really belong together," Tessa said glumly.

"Evan said Micah is in love with you, Tessa," Randi disclosed quietly.

Tessa shook her head fervently. "He's not. He knew it wouldn't last—"

"Things change," Randi interrupted. "Just like you never knew you'd fall for him, maybe he didn't realize it, either, when you were first together."

"But he . . . left." Tessa was afraid to hope that Micah felt even a portion of the love she knew she felt for him.

"You told him you didn't need him anymore. You told him he could go. How is he supposed to take that? Was he supposed to confess his love after you blew him off?" Randi paused before adding, "I know you two were at cross-purposes, but I have a feeling he concluded that you wanted him to leave. That's what Evan said."

"Oh, God. It isn't the way I meant it. I just knew if I didn't give him an out, I might do something stupid." Tessa sighed nervously.

Was it really possible Micah had misunderstood? "The last thing I'd ever want to do is hurt him, Randi," Tessa said tearfully, large droplets beginning to pour down her cheeks. "Meeting him changed my life."

"I know that," Randi replied as she held out a box of tissues to Tessa.

Tessa pulled a few from the container and wiped her eyes. "Maybe I can talk to him in New York. He'll be at the performance."

"You're going to discuss your relationship during a large event like that?"

Tessa shrugged. "What else can I do? I can hardly go to New York and throw myself at him. I don't even know where he lives, and I doubt they'd let me through the door."

Randi reached out and placed a supportive hand on her forearm. "Why can't you go to New York? I know where he lives. And all you have to do is have the doorman call up to his place and he can get you in."

"Maybe I should just text him—"

"No! Micah will bullshit you . . . I guarantee it. He's an arrogant, prideful Sinclair. You're going to have to go, and you're going to have to be pushy to get him to be honest with you. One of you is going to have to put yourself out there, risk rejection if you want to get a reward."

Tessa pointed at herself. "Me?"

"Since your rejection caused the problem, then yeah. It will probably have to be you. Micah thinks you wanted him to go. I doubt he'll put his ass on the line again until he has some reassurance. Men are funny that way." Randi paused before adding, "We do dumb things when we're hurt, Tessa, especially when it's somebody we love so much that we can't stand the pain. Evan and I almost lost each other over a stupid misunderstanding. I was so hurt that I forgot everything, including how much he meant to me. Don't let that happen to you."

"What if he still rejects me?" Tessa said nervously.

"Is he worth it?" Randi questioned.

"Oh, yeah," Tessa answered quickly. Micah was one man who was worth risking it all. "I think not knowing is worse than having to give up completely because we can't work things out. I've discovered that I'm not big on living with unknowns."

Tessa's brain was still whirling with the possibility that Micah really might care. Thinking back to their last conversation, it was possible that he'd felt rejected. She'd been the one who had brought up the subject of him leaving, and he hadn't ever really said he wanted to go. He'd simply agreed, his demeanor changing when she'd encouraged him to do what she thought he really wanted to do.

He'd left her two gifts, one of them the most amazing performance outfit she'd ever seen. It had been custom made by one of the best figure-skating designers in the country. To have it finished, Micah must have commissioned it almost from the minute she'd agreed to do the charity event. No doubt he'd taken sizes from her clothing at some point, because the ensemble fit perfectly. It was bright cherry red with gold embroidery and embellishments. Glamorous without being too gaudy.

The second item she was still wearing, and hadn't taken it off since she'd opened the jewelry box. The charm bracelet made of gold with beautiful matching charms was no ordinary piece of jewelry. Every gold charm meant something, a symbol of something they'd experienced together: an ice skate, a plane, a parachute, a dog that looked like Homer, a hiking boot, and two other charms that she wasn't quite sure how they fit in. The last two were a filigree heart and a golden rose. The bracelet and charms were beautifully crafted, and it spoke so much of things she'd experienced with Micah that she'd never been able to take it off. She knew she should send it back to him. It had to have been outrageously expensive, since it was solid gold with diamonds between the charms. But she hadn't been sure where to send it, and she'd fallen in love with it the minute she'd seen it nestled in a box of red velvet.

"Jared is getting his plane ready. You can drive right to the airport," Randi said excitedly as she clicked off her cell phone.

"I don't have anything with me." Tessa was still living in Micah's home, Randi's old place, but she'd been looking frantically for somewhere else to live.

"I'll put some stuff together for you, and you can shop there. You know you're loaded now, and you'll be in New York City," Randi told her adamantly.

"My skates and my outfit," Tessa protested. "In case I don't want to come back."

"Done. I'll pick them up for you and have them delivered to Micah's place," Randi offered.

"Thanks," Tessa answered, rising to her feet.

She waited, pacing the living room while Randi went and threw together a suitcase of necessities. They weren't exactly the same size, but close enough to make it work.

Unconsciously, she fingered the charm bracelet Micah had left her, putting her finger over the heart. What had he been trying to say by adding a heart and the rose?

"God, I was so stupid," she choked out on a sob, knowing in her heart that they were things that Micah hoped would be their future.

She'd panicked, knowing she'd fallen so deeply in love with Micah that she couldn't breathe. In a moment of uncertainty, she'd let him go, even though he'd never mentioned ending their relationship. It had been she who had been afraid of rejection, thinking she could save herself some heartache and embarrassment by cutting their ties so Micah could be free like she assumed he wanted to be.

While giving him what she assumed he wanted, she'd hurt him.

"Here you go," Randi said as she sailed back into the living room and stopped in front of her, shaking Tessa from her thoughts. "This will hold you until you can shop."

Tessa let her put the bag on the floor and then she hugged her friend tightly. "Thank you."

Randi squeezed her back before moving so Tessa could see her face. "You've been through so much. You know I wouldn't be doing this if I wasn't certain he cares," Randi explained, a thoughtful look on her face. "Evan and Micah are fairly close, and I trust Evan."

"I think he might be right," Tessa admitted. "I'm the one who got worried about being hurt. I chased him away. Even if it doesn't work, I have to try."

"You know Beatrice hasn't been wrong yet about a Sinclair," Randi teased. "I don't think she's wrong this time, either."

"Do you know what I love about him, Randi?" She loved almost everything about Micah, but one thing in particular.

"What?"

"He loves me just the way that I am. He doesn't see me as handicapped. It doesn't matter if I'm deaf. For him, it's just part of who I am, and he doesn't make it an issue at all. He never has. He sees right through my bullshit. It's like he can really *see* me. I guess he just wasn't looking at me the last time we spoke."

"Oh, Tessa. We all love you just the way you are. You're deaf, but you are still . . . you. I've known you since we were kids. Not being able to hear hasn't changed who you are here." Randi put her hand on her chest.

"I know. But Micah showed me that my fears were just fears. That they didn't define me, that my deafness didn't define me. I guess I never realized that until I met him. I finally know who I am, and I don't think I ever really knew myself until he challenged me to find out." Tessa knew she wasn't entirely fearless, especially since she'd messed up so badly with Micah. But she was determined to look what she dreaded in the face and fix it.

"Tell him that. Tell him exactly how you feel. If he can't handle it, then he isn't the man we think he is," Randi said, stepping back and squeezing Tessa's arm gently. "Do you want me to have Evan meet you there? I texted him while I was putting stuff together. He's sending a car to pick you up and take you to Micah's penthouse, but I know he'd be happy to be there for moral support."

Tessa thought for a moment and then slowly shook her head. It was tempting to have Evan escort her, have him around as a distraction or intermediary. "This is something I need to do alone."

"Then text me," Randi insisted. "I want to know you're there and safe."

She nodded at Randi, then collected her purse and extended the handle on the suitcase so she could pull it behind her.

When she patted her thigh, Homer got up from his watchful spot in the corner and sat by her side.

"I want to take Homer with me," Tessa decided.

"Take him. If I can take Lily to Asia, you can take Homer along to New York. Besides, he gets free entry anywhere. He's a service dog."

Luckily, Tessa had put Homer's doggie jacket on before leaving home because she'd wanted to stop a few places on the way to Randi's house. She had his special cover that marked him as a service dog.

Tessa hugged Randi one more time, grateful for all of the friends she had.

"I'll text Liam after I leave. He won't be happy. All he knows is that Micah went back to New York, but he doesn't believe that I broke it off."

Randi smirked. "I'll cover for you."

Tessa smiled back at her friend, remembering all the times they'd covered for each other when they were children. "I'll owe you one," she answered automatically, using the same expression they'd used as kids.

"I'll be sure to collect." It was the standard answer they both had used forever.

"I love you, Randi. So much. Thank you for always standing beside me." Tessa was beginning to learn that she never wanted to let an opportunity pass to tell the people she cared about how she felt. Randi had always been there for her, whether she wanted her to be or not. She was the one friend who had stampeded over Tessa's fears and hung on to her during her darkest times. How did you thank somebody for that?

"I love you like the sister I never had, Tessa. I always will." Randi hugged her with tears in her eyes, then pulled back. "Now go straighten out your stubborn Sinclair. Don't take *no* for an answer. Seduce him if you have to," Randi joked.

"I might do that first," Tessa answered, winking at her friend before she strode toward the door determinedly.

She had butterflies in her stomach as she left Randi's house, but she wasn't going to let anything stop her now. If there was a chance that she had hurt Micah, she was going to find out. *Her* feelings be damned.

Tessa could live with her pain, but the possibility of being the source of Micah's was more than she could bear.

CHAPTER 21

If Tessa had been in her right mind, she probably would have been awed by the luxury of Jared's private jet. It was definitely plush, with every convenience and every bit of comfort she could ever imagine.

Maybe if she'd been thinking properly, she also wouldn't have let Homer sit on one of the velvet seats, because he left dog hair everywhere. The attendant had told her it would be fine and she'd take care of it, but Tessa was a cleaner, and she hated making extra work for other people.

Unfortunately, her socially appropriate meter wasn't running, and she'd simply nodded and made her way to the car that Evan had sent to pick her up and take her to Micah's residence.

Once there, she stood on the sidewalk with Homer sitting by her side, her knuckles turning white from her grip on the suitcase handle.

I have to text him.

She looked up, and up, and then up some more. It wasn't even possible to see the floor where Micah made his home. The enormous, modern building had more stories than were even visible from the ground.

I can't just stand here forever.

The sun was starting to set, and she was being jostled by crowds coming from every direction. Stepping into a corner of the building by the entrance to keep out of the stream of human traffic, she dug her cell phone from her purse.

She sent the text determinedly.

Tessa: I need to talk to you. Please answer me.

She pressed the "Send" button and waited. It took him several tense minutes to answer.

Micah: I'm in New York and we've already said our goodbyes. What more is there to say?

Tessa: I never said goodbye and I have a lot to say. Can I come up, please?

Micah: You're here?

Tessa: Yes.

Micah: You came to New York City alone?

Tessa: No. I have Homer.

Micah: Alone! Wait right there. Don't move.

Tessa smiled, feeling her courage beginning to return as she realized he was worried about her being alone in the city.

She felt a light touch on her arm and she looked up to see the immaculately dressed doorman beside her. "Ms. Sullivan?" he asked, his expression polite.

"Yes."

"Mr. Sinclair asked me to see you inside."

She followed him, Homer on her heels.

She was led to what she assumed was a private elevator and stepped inside. The doorman pressed one of the buttons and gave her a dignified wave as he said, "Have a good evening, ma'am."

"You too," she squeaked out before the doors closed.

Fidgeting nervously, she watched as the elevator climbed, the numbers lighting up as it hit each floor. It didn't stop to pick up passengers, so she surmised that it was some kind of express elevator to the top. Her stomach dropped as it finally came to a stop.

The doors *whooshed* open, and right beyond the doors stood one of the best sights she'd seen in a long time.

Micah!

The only downside to having him right in front of her was that he looked angry. Really angry.

"What in fuck are you doing here? The performance isn't until next week, and you shouldn't be traveling to New York City alone." He reached out and grabbed her suitcase and then her hand, dragging her down the hallways until they reached the door to his residence.

He had a five-o'clock shadow that might have been a little more like six-o'clock instead. His feet were bare, and he had on a pair of worn jeans and a T-shirt that looked like it had been washed one too many times. Any trace of his usual humor had fled, and he dragged her into his penthouse and forcefully shut the door behind him.

"Talk," he demanded as he faced her. "You have something to say, then say it so I can get your ass back on my plane and make damn sure you get home safe."

She turned away from him and walked into the massive residence. The living room was right in front of her, so she took off the light jacket she was wearing and sat down on the couch.

Homer wagged his tail excitedly, nudging Micah for affection. The angry man patted the dog's head absently before walking over to stand beside the couch. "Comfortable?" His expression was wary and still pissed off.

"Yes, thank you," she answered politely, treading carefully.

"What do you want, Tessa?"

She held up her wrist. "What does the bracelet mean?"

"It really doesn't matter anymore."

"It matters to me," she argued.

"Why?"

"Because I love you," she blurted out, her heart racing as she lowered her arm. "I love you so much that I can't eat, I can't sleep, and I miss you more every minute that I'm not with you. I was hoping the heart on the bracelet meant something. I got to hoping it might mean that you wanted my heart someday. I came to tell you that you already have it. I think you have almost from the time we met."

The look on his face was brooding and cautious. "You fucking wanted me to leave."

She shook her head. "No. I didn't. I thought you wanted to go and I didn't want to hold you back. We both pretty much knew this was supposed to be a fling when it started, that we had to enjoy each other without getting attached. I knew the rules, but I also knew if you stayed much longer, I'd be begging you to stay forever, and you'd just feel worse about us parting. I never wanted you to go."

"Jesus Christ, Tessa. I can't do this." He turned his back and walked over to pour himself a drink.

Don't give up. Don't give up.

There weren't going to be any more misunderstandings. If he was going to reject her, he was going to do it completely.

She stood and started to remove her clothes, quickly dispensing of her shoes, her yoga pants, and underwear, and easily lifting her shirt over her head to add to the growing pile of clothing on the plush carpet.

She finished with the bra she was wearing, standing in his living room completely naked.

When he finally turned, he dropped the glass of Scotch he'd just poured on the floor with a roar. "What in the hell are you doing now?"

"I'm prepared to seduce you," she warned him. "But mostly I'm standing here bared to you completely. If you don't want me in your life, tell me directly, make me leave." She took a deep breath but didn't move. "I'm laying everything on the line right now, Micah. I love you more than I ever could imagine loving a man. You make me strong when I feel weak. You accept me just the way that I am. You make me a better person. My heart *is* yours. Take me or leave me. The choice is yours. I've already chosen *you* above anything else: hurt, pride, and fear."

She saw his big body shudder, then walk toward her, avoiding the glass on the floor. When he reached her, he put a hand on either side of her head. "You're a hell of a lot braver than I am. I ran from the house without explaining because I couldn't. I should have gone back, told you how I felt, but I was too damn destroyed, too worried about my own fucking heart. Oh, hell, yes, I love you. I love you more than it's healthy to love anybody. Every part of me craves you, Tessa: heart, body, and soul. Can you handle that? The way I feel about you won't make me an easy man to love."

She nodded as well as she could with him keeping her head still. "Quite easily. I love you the same way."

"How the fuck did this happen? You're never leaving me again," he demanded.

"You left me," she reminded him.

"Yeah, well, it's not happening again, because I don't plan on letting you go. The heart on the bracelet wasn't your heart, it was mine. I was hoping you'd get the hint that you had it."

"And the rose?"

"You'll figure that out soon enough."

"I love you," she whispered, her voice failing her as she looked into his ferocious eyes.

"I love you, too, sweetheart. You're mine. You were always meant to be mine. I feel it here." He moved one hand from her head to put it on his chest.

"I'm so sorry I hurt you," Tessa sobbed, her emotions out of control.

"Don't cry, Tessa. Please."

"I can't help it." She gulped, trying to contain her sobs of joy.

"Then I guess we need a distraction." He picked her up and tossed her over his shoulder, carrying her into a massive bedroom on the ground floor.

He dropped her gently on the bed and closed the door, and Tessa watched him in awe as he took off his clothes. Heat flooded between her thighs as he pulled the old T-shirt over his head, and she watched every muscle in his upper body flex.

As he tossed the garment to the floor, he said, "You didn't have to come here." He nodded to an overnight bag by the window of the bedroom. "I was coming back to Maine in the morning. I was willing to seduce you, too. I was ready to try anything to get you to stay with me."

Tessa's heart started to accelerate. "You were coming for me?"

"Yep. I kept trying to talk myself out of it, but I knew I was going to cave."

"I'm glad I came here. I wanted to tell you how much I loved you."

"I'm damn happy you did, too. I don't think I can keep getting myself off to fantasies of us together anymore. It's not helping." He popped the buttons on his jeans and pushed them down his legs, along with his boxer briefs. "I needed the real thing."

Tessa sighed as she viewed Micah in all his glory. Then, she held her arms out to him. "Come to me. I need you so much."

He strode to the bed and crawled after her like a stalking predator, his eyes dark and possessive.

This was obviously going to be on his terms, and Tessa was okay with that. Mutual need was about to consume them both.

He bodily lifted her up and dropped her down so her head hit the pillow, then he spread her legs and positioned himself between them. "I need to make you come, baby. Hard."

Before she could protest, his head was between her thighs, his wicked tongue stroking through her folds boldly, and Tessa let out a squeal of surprise. He devoured her like he hadn't had sustenance in weeks, using his mouth, nose, and tongue to consume her.

"Micah. Oh, God. Please. Fuck me now." She was desperate to have him buried inside her.

He ignored her, continuing to feast on her pussy until Tessa was thrashing on the bed, her hands gripping the silken coverlet.

She moaned as he slammed two fingers into her channel, using the digits to mimic what he planned on doing to her very shortly with his cock.

Tessa fisted his hair, jerking violently on the strands to pull him deeper, closer, her entire body quivering with ecstasy. This was no gentle climax approaching; it was a tidal wave of pent-up need that had been haunting her night and day since she'd last seen Micah.

Suddenly, he lifted his head and covered her body with his. "Next time, baby. Right now, we come together."

Her body hot and frustrated, she wrapped her legs around his hips as he plunged deep inside her, dragging a moan from her lips.

"You're mine, Tessa. Say it," he commanded, his face tense with fierce desire.

"I'm yours. I'll always be yours, Micah." She was panting as he pumped hard and fast into her slick sheath like a man possessed.

"Jesus, you feel so damn good, sweetheart," he told her right before he kissed her, claiming her lips with just as much fervor as he was claiming the rest of her body.

Their tongues dueled as their bodies were screaming toward release. Tessa met his marauding tongue stroke for stroke, and his invading cock with every pump of his hips.

She felt consumed, claimed, and loved.

"Micah. I can't hold it back." Her impending orgasm was so strong it was already pounding through her belly and to her core.

"Don't hold back. Let go. I'll be here to catch you when you fall," Micah replied, his mouth running fiercely over the skin at her neck, then finally biting hard enough to leave a mark.

Tessa's back arched from the pleasurable pain of his bite, a carnal act that she was sure he'd apologize for later, but seemed so natural during their desperate coupling.

Her fingernails tore into his back, Tessa feeling just as feral as Micah as her climax ripped through her. She screamed as the orgasm went on and on, watching Micah's face as he finally spilt his warm release deep inside her.

Rolling to her side, he gathered her into his arms, sheltering her, protecting her.

"I love you." The words burst from her mouth as she shivered with the lingering bliss of her climax.

Micah kissed her tenderly before replying, "I love you, too." He kissed her forehead gently.

They fell asleep a few moments later, their exhaustion both mental and physical.

Tessa sighed as she succumbed to slumber, knowing her life would never be the same.

It would be much, much better.

CHAPTER 22

"You look beautiful, baby. Are you nervous?"

Tessa adjusted the gorgeous skating ensemble she was wearing, knowing it was the most elegant performance costume she'd ever owned. The bright red was bold, and the elegant gold embellishments were classic. She was wearing her favorite tan custom skates to complement the outfit.

She smiled at Micah. "Surprisingly, I'm not at all. I guess the atmosphere feels normal to me." She stopped as she fingered her bracelet. "I wonder if I should take this off."

The jewelry was delicate, and wouldn't interfere with her skating. But she didn't want to lose it.

"Leave it. It has a strong safety clasp, and I'll buy you something else if it falls off."

Since she loved the comforting feel of knowing she was wearing something Micah had given her, she left it on. But she wasn't as nonchalant as he was at the thought of losing it. "It's almost time."

Earlier in the week, Micah had managed to get her ice time at the same stadium they were in right now. It had given her an opportunity to keep running through her routine. She was nowhere near the

Olympic-champion-level skater she'd been almost a decade ago, but she was also older, pretty much over the hill for a female figure skater. She smiled, knowing that for an old lady figure skater, she could pull off a respectable performance.

The last several days hadn't been all practice. Once they'd finally gotten out of bed, Micah had taken her to see the sights: the Empire State Building, the Statue of Liberty, and the 9/11 Memorial had been their first stops, Micah teasingly saying he felt like a tourist instead of an actual New Yorker. She'd let him feed her junk food from some of his favorite places to eat; the most memorable were Coney dogs from a street vendor.

In so many ways, it had been a magical week. Not only had she enjoyed her trip to New York immensely, but she'd been able to share all of those things with Micah.

"Ready?" he asked, looking more nervous than she was.

She reached for his hand and nodded, leading him toward the exit of the small preparation room.

She couldn't hear the madness of the crowd as they approached the area where she'd wait her turn, but she knew it was probably loud. People were screaming from the stands, standing up every time the skater on the ice landed a jump.

Knowing she was up next, she took the covers off her blades, smiling as she saw so many of her friends sitting in the front row. She bent down to hug each one of them. All of the Sinclairs were present with their wives. Jason and Hope also had a front-row seat beside Liam, the chair next to her brother sadly empty, even though Tessa knew that Micah had given her brother two tickets.

Beatrice and Elsie had Julian between them, Micah's brother having no choice but to listen to them.

"Beatrice, I think you can have these back now," Micah told the elderly woman as Tessa hugged her.

Beatrice blinked at him in surprise as she held out her hand to receive the two Apache tear stones from his hand. "Why, yes. It does look like you two don't need them anymore." She winked knowingly at Micah, and he smiled back at her.

Beatrice promptly gave one of the rocks to Julian, then reached across him to give the other one to Kristin. "I think they're going to the right place now."

Tessa looked at Micah, then watched the expressions of horror on Julian's and Kristin's faces as they tried to give the stones back to Beatrice. She was having none of it, so they both put the rocks in their pockets without looking at each other.

Julian and . . . Kristin?

Tessa thought they were an unlikely pair, since they didn't even get along, but no more unusual than her and Micah. She was learning to respect Beatrice's wisdom without questioning it anymore. Really, she almost wished the elderly woman had given one of those stones to Liam, but she guessed that it still wasn't his time.

She took a deep breath before she walked to the door that led out to the ice.

"Everything will be fine, Tessa," Micah said, carefully tugging her head back using the French braid that had been carefully crafted not long ago.

Micah kissed her, careful not to mess up her hair or smudge her makeup.

When they surfaced, she replied, "I know it will be. Everything I do, every move I make during the performance, I'm doing for you."

This skate would be a celebration of the happiness she'd found with Micah. Maybe they hadn't figured everything out, but it didn't matter.

"That's your cue, sweetheart." Micah nodded subtly at the ice.

She knew they'd just called her name, and she stepped out onto the slick surface, taking a warm-up lap before taking her posed position facing Micah.

All she had to do was wait for his signal to start.

I love you. He mouthed the words right before giving her the okay to start.

It seemed so strange for her world to be completely silent when she knew, between the arena and viewers on the TV, she had millions of people watching her. There was a full audience, yet she couldn't hear a single one of them yelling or clapping from the stands.

Peace flowed over her soul as she got caught up in the joy of skating, her movements flowing as she set up for her first jump combination.

She landed the two jumps in succession flawlessly, effortlessly, growing more confident as she made move after move without a problem.

Checking Micah's signals, she knew that she was flowing with the music, even as she picked up the tempo, doing a few choreographed sassy little moves as the speed of her routine grew faster.

Throughout the performance, she skated with happiness, a joy like she'd never experienced, trying to use her body to convey her emotions.

I have a man who loves me exactly as I am.

That realization freed her, elevated her until she felt like she was flying as she leapt into the air for her final jump, landing it lightly and perfectly.

She was panting and out of breath as she finished the routine with her usual flamboyant stance, holding the position for a moment before she covered her face with her hands and cried.

I did it. I finished without a flaw.

She made a small circle, her hands still over her face. Then, she made herself move her hands and started waving to a crowd who were all on their feet, even though everything was silent.

The air in the stadium vibrated with enthusiasm and excitement. She couldn't hear it, but she could *feel* it.

Tessa startled as a body slammed against her, and she turned quickly only to realize it was Micah. He was on his skates, an enormous bouquet of roses in his arms.

"These are for you," he told her, laying all but one carefully on the ice. "This one is from me."

She reached out to take it with a tearful smile on her face, not noticing there was something attached as she accepted the gift from him. Then, when she had it in her hand, she saw it. Simultaneously, Micah dropped onto the ice on one knee, looking up at her.

He started to sign, putting emphasis on every movement he made. *I. Love. You. You bared yourself completely to me, and now I'm doing the same thing. Please put me out of my misery and marry me. Be with me forever. I promise I'll stay beside you whatever our future holds.*

She looked from him to the rose in her hand, realizing that there was a beautiful diamond ring on the stem of the flower.

She looked at him with her heart in her eyes, knowing he was risking everything by coming out here in front of millions of people and placing his heart in her hands. He was willing to make himself as vulnerable to her as she had to him. He was just doing it in a different way.

"Oh, my God." Tessa put a hand over her face and started to cry again, her heart racing with excitement and her nerves so raw that she couldn't help but cry.

"Don't cry, Tessa." Micah rose up as he signed.

She dropped her hands and gaped at him. "You really want to marry me?"

He grinned. "I really, really do." He nodded to the crowd. "I think they just realized that you're deaf. They're so loud that I can't hear a thing."

"Welcome to my world," she answered with an enormous expression of joy on her face.

Micah reached out and slid the ring down the stem and held it out to her. "Well, I'm making a total ass out of myself right now. Are you going to marry me or not?"

Her hand trembled as she stuck it out. "How can I say no? There are millions of people watching," she teased.

"Don't say yes because you think you have to. Say yes only if you want this as much as I do," Micah answered with a grim expression.

"Then, yes. Yes. Yes. Yes." She told him happily, "I want to be with you forever. I can't imagine my life without you in it."

"I don't want to imagine life without you, Tessa," Micah answered as he slid the gorgeous diamond on her finger.

She admired it for a moment, the beautiful platinum band with an enormous diamond in the center and a circle of smaller stones around the centerpiece.

Tessa took the rose and flung herself at her new fiancé, a man so strong and powerful, yet so vulnerable at the same time. "I love you," she told him before she hugged him tightly.

He tipped her chin up, his eyes a stormy sea of emotions as he wrapped his arms around her waist. "Your devoted audience is chanting for a kiss."

"Then don't disappoint them," she murmured, staring back at him lovingly.

He swooped down and kissed her, right there in front of millions of people, but he didn't seem to care. He kissed her until she was breathless again, her heart ready to burst from her chest.

When he finally released her, he advised, "Wave to your crowd, sweetheart. They're going crazy. They all adore you, especially now that they know that even with challenges to overcome, you skated like an angel. You were amazing."

She faced the audience in each direction, waving enthusiastically with an ecstatic expression that she couldn't hide even if she wanted to.

Young skaters were coming to collect the flowers that had been thrown onto the ice by fervent observers as Micah took her hand and led her slowly to the exit.

He held the door open and allowed her to get out of the rink first. She nearly bumped into the next performer. "I'm so sorry," she muttered, looking up as she apologized.

She cringed as she saw Rick standing behind one of her former female competitors, Shannon, a woman she'd never liked because of her cruelty to all of the other women in her profession. The female skater had medaled in the same Olympics that Tessa had; she'd gotten the bronze.

"Theresa," the dark-haired female acknowledged. "You could watch where you're going."

"Now, darling. Don't get upset. She is dealing with a handicap," Rick said rudely.

Micah moved in front of her. "Shut the fuck up or I'll lay you out on the floor in so much pain, you'll wish you were dead."

Tessa moved to Micah's side. "Don't." She grabbed his hand. "He's not worth it."

"Aiming your aspirations a little low, aren't you, Sinclair?" Rick asked drily.

Micah lunged and grasped Rick by the collar of his polo shirt. "Honestly, I think she's way too good for me, but for some reason she wants to marry me anyway," Micah said with what appeared to be a growl. "Get the fuck out of my event."

"I have a ticket. I came to see my new girlfriend skate," Rick protested.

Shannon ignored the two men when her name was called and stepped out onto the ice. Then, as she approached the middle of the rink, she got tripped up and fell on her ass before she'd even started her routine.

Tessa bit her lip to keep from smiling.

Is it so bad of me to be happy that an old member of my team took a fall?

Her ex-teammate got to her feet with a volatile look on her face, and Tessa decided she didn't care if she was being bad or not. She smiled.

Micah pulled his arm back and smashed Rick hard in the face, watching as the man hit the floor. "There. Now both you and your girlfriend have fallen on your asses," Micah said with a smirk. "Karma can really be a bitch sometimes," he added nonchalantly. "Enjoy the show. I've seen everything I care about."

Tessa followed Micah back to the preparation room they'd been in before the performance. He tugged her inside and closed the door behind him.

She found herself immediately boxed in, Micah pinning her to the door. "How in the hell did you ever put up with that jackass?"

Honestly, now Tessa didn't know exactly why she'd stayed with Rick for so long. "Maybe because he was all I ever knew," she said breathlessly, looking into the eyes of the man who would belong to her forever. "I didn't know what love was back then."

"So you think you do now?" he asked cautiously.

"Yes. It's a man who sees me as beautiful no matter what. It's a man who challenges me and doesn't treat me like I'm different or like I have limitations. It's a man who is willing to make himself vulnerable to me, even though it's not a comfortable position at all for a powerful man to be in." Tessa sighed. "For me, that's you, my love."

His expression still fierce, he leaned his forehead against hers and rested there for a moment before he lifted his head again.

"You *are* beautiful. But you *are* different—different from any woman I've ever known. You were amazing tonight, Tessa. Not amazing *considering you're deaf.* You were *just* amazing."

Her heart thumped as he gazed down at her with a look of love in his eyes, an expression that she hoped would never go away. She said, "I wonder why it is that you showed up just when I needed you so much, just when I was ready."

He grinned. "Because Beatrice's stone cleared our pathway?" he asked.

"Maybe. I can almost believe that we were thrown together now for a reason. Maybe I wasn't ready before. But I am now."

She circled her arms around his neck and urged him down to her.

"How ready?" he asked almost hesitantly.

"Very ready," she concluded, her expression sensual.

He grasped her ass and pulled her body against him. "Show me," he insisted.

He was challenging her, and she knew she was in trouble. "Okay," she agreed, knowing she'd always rise to his challenges—simply because she wanted to.

And so, right there in the tiny room, she did everything she could to rock his world. She let go of any inhibitions she had, her adrenaline still pumping through her body from her performance and Micah's proposal.

A little while later, completely sated, Micah declared defeat and told her he was completely persuaded that she really was ready to open her heart completely, and he was damn grateful for that.

EPILOGUE

A Few Weeks Later

Tessa looked slowly around the enormous, ridiculously ornate table, realizing that everyone she really cared about was here. Micah had wanted a Vegas wedding, but then backed down because he thought she deserved the wedding of her dreams.

Little did he realize, *he* was her dream. She hadn't cared about the wedding just as long as they had family and friends attending. So once she'd convinced Micah that it didn't matter to her where they got married, there was no stopping him.

They'd wed in one of the prettiest chapels in Las Vegas, and the wedding dinner she was currently attending had everybody present that she really needed. Liam was here, seated right across from Micah. Dante, Grady, Jared, Jason, and Evan were all sitting next to their wives, and Julian was sitting next to Kristin, the two of them appearing to be in an argument, a common occurrence for those two these days.

Tessa sighed, and Micah squeezed her hand under the table. She turned and looked at him, still astonished that she was now married to this wonderful man who had changed her life in so many ways.

"Having second thoughts?" he joked.

She shook her head. "Not for even an instant. I was just thinking that just about everything that matters to me is here."

Micah's expression turned more serious. "Me too."

"I'm so sorry Xander couldn't be here," she told him softly. Micah's brother was, thankfully, still in the rehab center.

"I'm not. I'm damn grateful he's still in rehab. Hopefully he'll stay there. It's the best wedding gift he could give me." He hesitated before asking, "Are you nervous about going back to New York?"

Tessa was returning to New York with Micah to start her implant procedure. They'd stay there for a while as she went through the process and Micah tried to rearrange the hierarchy in his company to function better with him living out of state. If he'd wanted to, she would have stayed with him in New York in a heartbeat. But Micah being Micah, he'd told her that location didn't matter to him, and he liked Amesport. The builders on his property had made great progress, and he wanted to make Amesport his home, even though it would mean some frequent trips to New York for business.

She looked up into his eyes, her heart tripping as she noticed his worried expression. A man in a tuxedo shouldn't look so serious. Especially not a man like Micah. Neither one of them had changed clothing, and she was still wearing the glorious wedding dress she'd purchased when they were in New York.

Lifting her palm to his cheek, she explained, "I'm not afraid, Micah. It's not a dangerous procedure, and I know you won't stop loving me if I'm not perfect or the implants aren't successful for some reason."

"You're already fucking perfect," he told her, a stubborn expression on his face. "I don't give a shit if you don't hear my voice."

Stroking a finger down his cheek, she said, "I already know your voice. I hear it in my head every day, sometimes when you aren't even in the same room with me. For me, you already have a voice. It's kind, bold, sometimes arrogant, but always sexy."

"Good." He nodded. "But what happens if I sound like a dick when you get your hearing back again?" He lifted a brow as he stared at her.

Tessa snorted. "Your voice doesn't come from here." She touched his mouth. "It comes from here." She touched his heart. "And here." She touched his temple. "And maybe a little bit from here." She took her hand from his under the table and trailed her fingers up his thigh and to his cock. Then she squeezed the already-erect member with her fingers, smiling sweetly at him at the same time.

"You'll pay later, woman," Micah warned her.

"Oh, I hope so," she replied, slowly taking her hand away from his groin and joining their fingers together again.

"I think it's time to find our honeymoon suite."

Tessa chuckled. "We haven't even eaten yet."

Payback!

He shot her a hungry look that had nothing to do with food and everything to do with making *her* his dinner as he said, "I'll eat what I want in the suite."

He tore his eyes away to look across the table, and he squeezed her hand as Randi stood and tapped her spoon on her champagne glass, asking for silence.

Tessa found it amusing that for her, *everything* was *already* dead quiet.

She watched as Randi straightened her dress, then looked directly at Tessa as she spoke and signed her words. "Evan and Julian don't want to speak, so I'm doing the newlywed toast. Tessa and I have known each other since we were kids. Because she was so dedicated to figure skating, she didn't have a normal childhood or adolescence. I've watched her triumphs and then her heartache, something she took with more courage than I think I would have if I were her. She's resilient, talented, and she deserves every bit of happiness she has right now with Micah. I was always happy to have her back, and always grateful to have her stand behind me when I needed her. So here's to one of the kindest, most faithful friends I've ever known. Here's to Tessa and Micah. We all wish you as much happiness as we've found." Randi reached down for Evan's hand, then picked up and raised her glass as everyone else did the same.

Julian stood. "To Micah and Tessa. I love you both, bro, or there's no way I'd have flown here before I had to fly away to another damn movie shoot." He lifted his glass and drained it as everyone else sipped from their glasses.

Kristin grabbed the edge of Julian's tuxedo jacket and jerked him back into his seat.

Tessa stood and walked around the table to Randi, giving her a huge hug for her sweet words before returning to her seat.

"What's wrong with Julian? He doesn't look happy," she asked Micah as she sat back down. "And why are he and Kristin having words again? Why does he dislike her so much?"

Tessa wasn't close enough to see what they were saying, but she could tell from the irritated expressions on Julian's and Kristin's faces that whatever they were saying wasn't pleasant.

"I have no idea," Micah answered. "But I don't think he exactly dislikes her. Just the opposite, I suspect."

Tessa's eyes left Micah's face and she looked at Julian and Kristin again. Granted, Beatrice had given them the stones, but surely that wasn't going to happen if they disliked each other so much . . .

Micah put a hand on her arm. "Don't worry about them. They'll figure it out. Besides, Julian's on my shit list right now. He told me that he was the one who informed the Fund where to find you. It seems that he recognized you the first time he saw you. In his defense, he didn't know that you didn't skate anymore, and he thought he was doing a good thing for both you and the Sinclair Fund. But I'd still like to kick his ass for outing your location."

"He recognized me?" That surprised Tessa. "I'm not angry at him. I'm glad. I owe him. That invitation led to a lot of good things for me," she told Micah with a sultry smile.

He nodded toward the plates being placed in front of them. "Our dinner is here. Eat well. I might not let you out of our suite for a while."

All it took was that single comment for Tessa to be unable to clear her mind of sensual images all through dinner, and then again during the wedding cake.

She laughed as Homer stuck his head out from under the table, reminding her that he was there as she ate her cake. Her furry friend had a sweet tooth, and she snuck him a bite of the cake, sticking her hand under the table as the canine quickly devoured the sweet treat and licked her fingers.

Watching as Homer moved from her side and situated himself between her and Micah, she saw her new husband do exactly the same thing she'd done, except he'd slipped her dog nearly an entire piece of the sugary treat.

No matter how much Micah tried to play the tough guy, his *heart* would never be hard. He was a guy who had as many facets as the beautiful diamond on her finger, every one of them special, every one part of him. Combined, they made up the man that Micah was now, and she loved every one of those sides of the man she'd married.

He nudged her and she looked up at him as she dropped her fork on her empty plate.

Tilting her chin, he said, "Everybody wants a kiss."

Looking around, Tessa could see everybody tapping their spoons on their water glasses, demanding that Micah kiss his new bride.

The feel of his warm breath on her face, and the hot, sexy scent he gave off as he stroked her chin, made her lean closer to him. "I never did like to disappoint an audience," she murmured.

"I don't care about everybody else. Kiss me," he demanded.

His arrogant, bossy side was hard to resist, so she didn't even bother. She leaned closer and kissed him.

She couldn't hear the whoops of approval as her mouth collided with Micah's. All she recognized was the now-familiar sense of euphoria whenever they touched, Micah's total commitment to them as a couple, and mostly, his love. And for Tessa, hearing *Micah's voice* was more than enough.

~ The End ~

ACKNOWLEDGMENTS

My sincerest thanks to my amazing street team, Jan's Gems, for everything you do for me to spread the word about my books. You ladies are truly amazing.

Rita, thank you for always being so willing to help me out. Your friendship as well as your editing skills make you one of my greatest assets.

Thank you to my Senior Editor, Maria Gomez, and all of the Montlake team for your continued support of The Sinclairs. This series is an incredible journey for me, and I'm glad I'm sharing it with the entire Montlake Romance team.

To my own KA team: Sandie, Annette, Isa, Natalie, Tami, and Sri. I'm only as strong as the team behind me, and all of you keep me going, even during the most challenging of times. I love you all. I'm not sure how I got so lucky to have such an awesome group of employees, but I must have done something good to deserve all of you. Thank you for being the very best support system a woman could ever have.

As always, thank you to my readers, who allow me to do what I love to do. You'll never know how much your comments, letters, and excitement about my books really mean to me, so I'll just say thank you to every one of you once again.

xxx Jan (J.S. Scott)

ABOUT THE AUTHOR

 *Photo © 2013 by Carrie Herzog* J.S. "Jan" Scott is a *New York Times, USA Today*, and *Wall Street Journal* bestselling romance author. She's an avid reader of all types of books and literature, but romance has always been her genre of choice. Writing what she loves to read, Jan pens both contemporary and paranormal romances. They are almost always steamy, they generally feature an alpha male, and they include a happily ever after because she just can't seem to write them any other way! Jan lives in the beautiful Rocky Mountains with her husband and two very spoiled German Shepherds.

Jan loves to connect with readers.

You can visit her at:

Website: http://www.authorjsscott.com

Facebook: http://www.facebook.com/authorjsscott

You can also tweet @AuthorJSScott

For updates on new releases, sales, and giveaways, please sign up for Jan's newsletter by going to: http://eepurl.com/KhsSD